Wade was jealous!

The thought sent a tingly thrill up Anne's spine. She opened her mouth to deny he had any right to be jealous. But no words would form while he was so close.

"Why do you wear those clothes?" he asked.

"What's wrong with my clothes? I shop at good stores."

"They're baggy. I think you dress to keep men away." He placed one hand against the wall on either side of her, not quite touching her. "And I think you wear your hair slicked back for the same reason." He grabbed the end of her braid and removed the elastic band. Immediately the braid started to unravel.

"Then it's not working very well, is it?" Her voice sounded thready, pleading. She did not want to face this...this *need* she had, so unseemly, so *not* her.

"Tell me you don't want to get back what we had."

She couldn't.

"Didn't think so." With that, Wade claimed the kiss he'd been inching toward.

Dear Reader,

It's hot outside. So why not slip into something more comfortable, like a delicious Harlequin American Romance novel? This month's selections are guaranteed to take your mind off the weather and put it to something much more interesting.

We start things off with Debbi Rawlins's *By the Sheikh's Command*, the final installment of the very popular BRIDES OF THE DESERT ROSE series. Our bachelor prince finally meets his match in a virginal beauty who turns the tables on him in a most delightful way. Rising star Kara Lennox begins a new family-connected miniseries, HOW TO MARRY A HARDISON, and these sexy Texas bachelors will make your toes tingle. You'll meet the first Hardison brother in *Vixen in Disguise*—a story with a surprising twist.

The talented Debra Webb makes a return engagement to Harlequin American Romance this month with *The Marriage Prescription*, a very emotional story involving characters you've met in her incredibly popular COLBY AGENCY series from Harlequin Intrigue. Also back this month is Leah Vale with *The Rich Girl Goes Wild*, a not-to-be-missed billionaire-in-disguise story.

Here's hoping you enjoy all we have to offer this month at Harlequin American Romance. And be sure to stop by next month when Cathy Gillen Thacker launches her brand-new family saga, THE DEVERAUX LEGACY.

Best,

Melissa Jeglinski
Associate Senior Editor
Harlequin American Romance

VIXEN IN DISGUISE

Kara Lennox

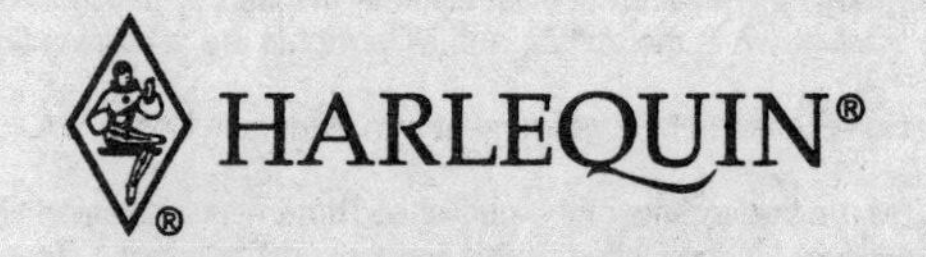

TORONTO • NEW YORK • LONDON
AMSTERDAM • PARIS • SYDNEY • HAMBURG
STOCKHOLM • ATHENS • TOKYO • MILAN • MADRID
PRAGUE • WARSAW • BUDAPEST • AUCKLAND

ISBN 0-373-16934-5

VIXEN IN DISGUISE

This edition published by arrangement with Harlequin Books S.A.

Visit us at www.eHarlequin.com

Printed in U.S.A.

ABOUT THE AUTHOR

Texas native Kara Lennox has been an art director, typesetter, advertising copy writer, textbook editor and reporter. She's worked in a boutique, a health club and has conducted telephone surveys. She's been an antiques dealer and briefly ran a clipping service. But no work has made her happier than writing romance novels.

When Kara isn't writing, she indulges in an ever-changing array of weird hobbies, from rock climbing to crystal digging. But her mind is never far from her stories. Just about anything can send her running to her computer to jot down a new idea for some future novel.

Books by Kara Lennox

HARLEQUIN AMERICAN ROMANCE

840—VIRGIN PROMISE
856—TWIN EXPECTATIONS
871—TAME AN OLDER MAN
893—BABY BY THE BOOK
917—THE UNLAWFULLY WEDDED PRINCESS
934—VIXEN IN DISGUISE*

*How To Marry a Hardison

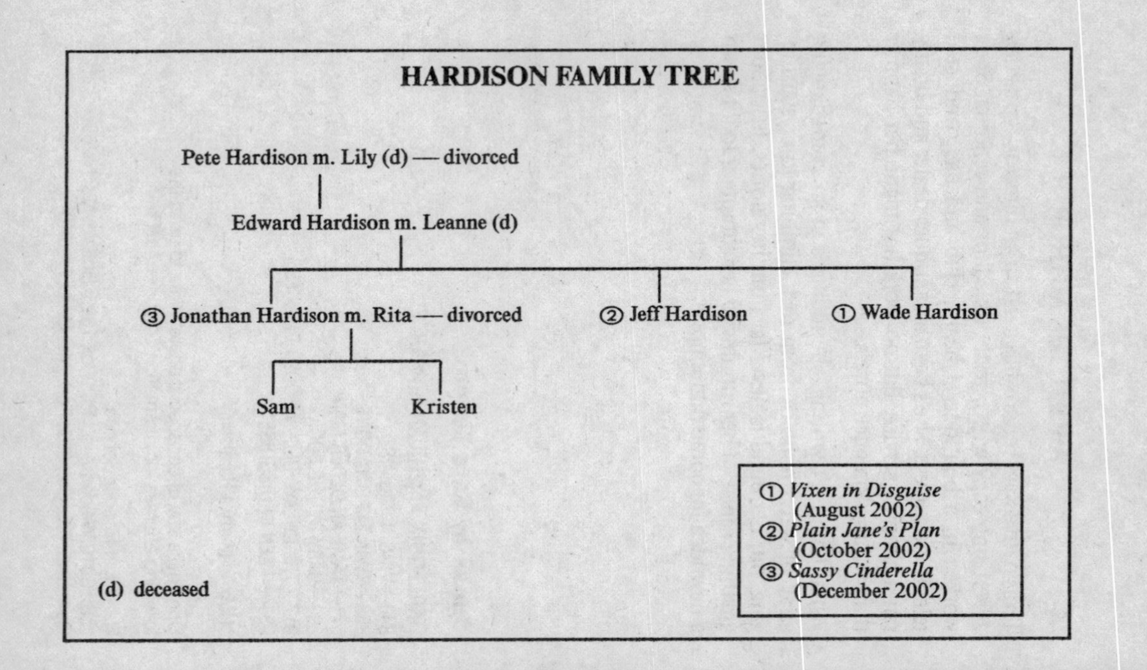
HARDISON FAMILY TREE
Pete Hardison m. Lily (d) — divorced
Edward Hardison m. Leanne (d)
③ Jonathan Hardison m. Rita — divorced
② Jeff Hardison
① Wade Hardison
Sam
Kristen
① Vixen in Disguise (August 2002)
② Plain Jane's Plan (October 2002)
③ Sassy Cinderella (December 2002)
(d) deceased

Chapter One

The Autumn Daze Festival in Cottonwood, Texas, hadn't changed a bit in thirteen years, Wade Hardison thought as he strolled down Elm Street. The usually sleepy town square had been temporarily transformed into a whirling kaleidoscope of sensory overload.

Bands of screaming children streaked past him, their exuberant laughter plucking nostalgic chords in Wade's mind. PTA mothers and their farmer husbands did good imitations of circus barkers, luring townsfolk and tourists alike to try their luck at the ringtoss or the dunking booth, where Mayor Dilly was currently the victim.

Smells of popcorn, cotton candy and barbecued turkey legs filled the air, reminding Wade he was hungry. He tried to make up his mind what to eat as dusk slowly descended on the crisp fall day. Yards and yards of twinkling white lights flickered to life.

It was good to be home. Wade had left Cottonwood as an angry adolescent, at odds with everybody, unsure of his place in the world, but ready to go out and conquer it. He'd done what he set out to do—he'd carved a niche for himself and become the best at something his brothers knew nothing about. He'd returned far mellower, ready to make peace with his family.

Only problem was, he wasn't sure his family wanted to make peace with him. When he'd left, he'd been concerned only with his own perceived wounds, positive his family would be happy to see the last of him. He'd had no idea the scars he'd left behind. His homecoming two days ago had been awkward at best, and certainly no one had dragged out the fatted calf.

But at least his grandfather had let him stay at the ranch house.

When he caught sight of a redhead leaning against an ancient live oak, working cautiously at a caramel apple, Wade thought for a moment his heart had stopped. Then he thought he must be hallucinating.

Though he hadn't seen Annie since last May, he hadn't forgotten one thing about her—not her laugh or her scent or the feel of her hand in his. He'd had to make do with memories because they were all he had—she'd left him, disappeared without a word.

Now, when he least expected it, here she was, in his hometown of all places. At least, he thought it was her. Same red hair. Same big green eyes. Same luscious mouth, which, as he watched, did intriguing things to the caramel apple she nibbled on. She paused now and then to lick her lips and delicately blot them with a paper napkin.

But some things about her weren't like Annie at all. Her hair, for instance. The color was right, but Annie's bouncy curls were wild and barely controlled, a tangle of deep-red silk a man could lose himself in.

This woman's hair had been slicked into a severe knot at the back of her head.

And the clothes were all wrong. Annie had worn tight jeans, a clingy shirt with a low neckline, a vest with rhinestone studs. Her fingers had been decorated with numerous rings, and she'd worn big, dangly earrings. This woman wore a loose turtleneck and a shapeless corduroy jumper, black stockings and loafers. Little gold studs in her ears.

The most dramatic difference between Annie and the mystery woman, however, was in the face. The features were the same, but the expression very different. Annie had smiled and laughed and teased all the time. This woman's face was tight, with a cautious look to the eyes. And he saw something else in her eyes, too—a sadness that couldn't be denied.

"See something you like?"

Wade jumped and nearly spilled his soft drink. His older brother Jeff had sidled up next to him, but Wade had been so fixated on the caramel-apple woman he hadn't even been aware of the intrusion.

Wade couldn't very well deny he'd been staring. "Who is she?"

"You don't remember her?"

"You know her, then." Dumb question. Jeff knew everybody. He'd gone to medical school, then into practice several years ago with their father, who'd been the town's only doctor for decades. Sooner or later everyone came in to see one of the Docs Hardison.

"Of course I know her. She's Milton Chatsworth's daughter."

Milton Chatsworth, their father's best friend from

college. Wade struggled to fit the memories into place. Milton had retired and moved his family to Cottonwood shortly before Wade had left town, but he remembered meeting him and his family at their fancy lake house.

Then the fuzzy picture snapped into focus. "I remember a scrawny, redheaded girl, all knock-knees and braces."

"That's the one. Don't bother her, okay?"

"What's her name?" Wade asked anxiously.

Jeff reluctantly complied. "Anne. She just graduated from law school at SMU, following in her old man's footsteps."

Wade hardly heard what Jeff was saying. He'd seized on the name, Anne. Annie. And Southern Methodist University was in Dallas, where he'd first met Annie.

He didn't believe in coincidence. Had to be the same woman. And he wasn't about to let her get away twice.

"Wade? Are you listening?" Jeff asked impatiently.

"Yeah, sure."

"She's got a lot to deal with right now. She doesn't need any extra grief."

That comment got Wade's dander up. He turned his full attention on his brother. "Why do you automatically assume I'll bring a woman grief? Maybe I could be the light of her life."

Jeff sighed. "If you'd lose that chip on your shoulder for thirty seconds, you'd realize I'm looking out for your best interests, too. I know Anne Chatsworth, and she's not your type."

Wade allowed a slow smile to win over his face. His temper, always quick to flare, just as quickly died away. He was no longer sixteen, and he didn't have to listen to his brothers or his father or grandfather anymore, telling him how to live his life. Just reminding himself of that fact eased the defensiveness he'd developed to survive as an average kid in a family of overachievers.

He looked his brother squarely in the eye. "I suspect you don't know Anne as well as you think you do."

With that he tipped his hat and turned toward Anne Chatsworth, intending to renew his acquaintance with her.

But she was gone.

"WOULD YOU THROW that nasty thing away?" Deborah Chatsworth said to her daughter as they walked along Livestock Lane, where the Future Farmers of America and 4-H Club kids displayed their prize animals in hopes of winning a blue ribbon for their trophy cases. "You don't have to keep gnawing on it like a dog with a bone."

Anne Chatsworth paused and looked at her half-eaten treat, then at her mother. "It's a caramel apple. You're supposed to gnaw on it."

"Well, it doesn't look very dignified."

"We're at a county fair, where people chase after greased pigs and the mayor lets himself be dunked in a tank fully clothed. Nobody's worried about dignity here."

"You can say that again."

Attending the Autumn Daze Festival hadn't been a

number-one priority for Deborah. She'd tried to get out of it, but Anne's father had insisted they go.

"I intend to run for town council next year," Milton Chatsworth had said earlier that day when both his wife and daughter had been reluctant to fight the crowds of tourists. "How would it look if I didn't attend the town's biggest event of the year?"

Anne thought it was kind of cute that her father, after years of insulating himself from the townies, had decided to venture forth from his lake house and get involved. "Come on, Mom, let's humor him," Anne had said, and Deborah had finally agreed to come along.

Anne was glad she'd come. Getting out of the house these last few weeks had become a chore for her. She recognized the signs of perfectly natural depression and knew that getting out and distracting herself was the best medicine. So she'd made herself get dressed and come to the fair, to please her father, because she really loved both her parents despite their lofty self-images.

Once she'd arrived at the fair, she'd gotten caught up with it, fondly remembering the festivals of her teen years, when she'd run with a gang of other kids she desperately wanted to fit in with, stuffing herself with cotton candy, riding the Ferris wheel, listening to the bands that played, usually badly, at the bandstand.

Life had been simpler then, and for just these few hours she'd been able to recapture that less complicated time. In fact, today, for the first time in almost a month, she'd felt as if she might be able to get on with her life, instead of just going through the motions and pretending, for her parents' sake, that she was okay.

"Now where do you suppose your father has gotten to?" Deborah asked.

Anne threw away the core of her caramel apple, thoroughly gnawed, and paused to stroke a cream-colored Shetland pony. "Maybe at the watermelon-seed-spitting contest?"

Deborah glowered at her daughter.

"Okay, I'll be serious. I think he said he'd been asked to judge something—pies or pickles, something like that."

Deborah looked exasperated. "The food is all the way on the other side of the square. I'm ready to go home, aren't you? You look pale."

"I feel fine, just a little tired." Her physical stamina was alarmingly low.

"Stay here, then. I'll go round up your father." Deborah gave Anne a solicitous pat and headed off in her pumps, her figure still slender and straight despite her sixty-five years. Anne smiled and shook her head. Only her mother would wear heels to a county fair.

The pony enjoyed Anne's attention, so she continued to pet it for a few minutes, its velvety nose soft against her palm.

"I've been looking all over for you."

That voice.

Anne tensed, then gasped and turned so quickly she startled the pony, which snorted and pranced away. For a few moments all she could do was stare at the apparition standing in front of her—far too close for sanity.

Wade Hardison. What was he doing here? She'd been certain that he was permanently estranged from his family, that the last place he would ever go was Cottonwood, Texas, so she'd never worried about a chance meeting with him.

Anne blinked a couple of times, but he was no hallucination. In fact, he was disturbingly real—solid-looking as a tree trunk, and every bit as devilishly handsome as the memories she conjured up on an hourly basis.

In the next heartbeat she schooled her features, controlled her breathing and decided how she would handle this.

"Excuse me?" she said, trying to look confused.

"If you say you don't remember me, my heart's gonna break in two right here."

"I—I'm sorry. You look slightly familiar, but I'm not good with names." That was a fat lie. When it came to names and faces, her mind was like flypaper. His face was etched into her memory with the permanency of Mount Rushmore.

Wade narrowed his eyes. "Familiar? *Slightly* familiar? I guess I'm just one of a long stream of guys you share passionate weekends with, huh, Annie?"

"I beg your pardon, sir, my name is not Annie. You obviously have me confused with someone else." An alternate persona that would never, ever see the light of day again, if Anne had anything to say about it. Hadn't her father always told her to be cautious? To never, ever trust strangers? And especially to never let common impulses and unchecked appetites rule her head?

"Anne, then, if you insist. Anne Chatsworth, newly minted lawyer."

"How do you know that?" she asked with some alarm.

"My brother told me."

Anne felt the blood drain to her feet, making her suddenly dizzy. Wade's brother Jeff. Dr. Jeff Hardison, her physician and a close family friend. How naive she'd been to trust that the Hardison family rift would never be healed. She knew Jeff would not reveal her medical details to anyone without her authorization, not for any reason, under any circumstances. He was an excellent doctor, and she had complete confidence in him. But the fact that Jeff and Wade had been discussing her at all…well, that was bad.

"You did me wrong, Annie."

"I am not Annie," she insisted. "I have no idea what you're talking about."

"Oh, I think you do." He grasped her arm and halted her attempted escape, then slid his fingers up to her shoulder.

"Please," she said, feeling panicky. He continued to touch her, his hand hot even through her shirt, though his grasp was loose. She could escape any time—if she could only make herself move. But her feet remained welded to the ground.

He leaned closer. "Please what?"

"I'm not Annie."

"Then why are you standing here about to let me kiss you?"

Lord help her, he was right. She stood in his light embrace, paralyzed like a deer in headlights by the look and feel of him, his scent. He had her mesmerized, just as he had the moment she'd laid eyes on him, when she was twelve and he was sixteen. And again, when she'd seen him for the first time in thirteen years, at the Mesquite Rodeo last spring. He had a strange power over her.

Her body quivered as he slowly closed the distance between them. She knew she should back away, push him, run, scream, anything but kiss him. Yet she stood there, her breath caught in her lungs, and allowed him to touch his mouth to hers, very gently, very sweetly. Like a first kiss, so tender it made her ache. She melted into it. She couldn't help herself. He tasted like coming home.

It lasted only a few seconds, and when he pulled away, he was smiling triumphantly. "Kisses don't lie, Annie. Now, are you going to tell me why you ran out on me without a word?"

Anne heard voices behind her. A small knot of fair goers were heading into the parking lot, sending her heart into overdrive. Her parents—what if they saw her? What if *anyone* saw her? She had to get out of here, for her sanity as well as a whole host of reasons.

"All right." She disentangled herself from Wade's warm embrace. Obviously, she hadn't fooled him into thinking he'd misidentified her. "I do owe you an apology and an explanation, and I'll give them to you, but not here, not now." She cast a nervous glance over her shoulder.

"Afraid to be seen with me?"

"Yes!" When his cocky grin slid away, she quickly added, "It's a complicated situation, but I'll explain it. Later."

"When?" he pressed.

"Tomorrow."

"Tonight."

"Okay, all right."

"Midnight."

"Eleven. I'll be in bed by midnight."

"I hope so." Wade's eyes burned like two hot coals.

She should have known better than to mention the word *bed.* Anne searched her brain for a private meeting place, but Wade provided one for her.

"At the ranch. The old red barn that's used to store hay. You know it?"

She nodded.

"I'll be waiting."

Again she nodded.

"If you don't show, I'll come find you." He turned and sauntered away.

Anne didn't doubt him. She also wouldn't blame him if he was really angry with her. But when she'd left him last May, it had seemed her only choice. She hadn't counted on an emotional entanglement when she'd set off for the Mesquite Rodeo in her borrowed cowgirl duds, eager to blow off some exam-induced steam.

Eleven. If she left the house late at night, her parents naturally would ask where she was going. The truth would just lead to a whole lot of questions she didn't want to answer. She would have to slip out under their radar.

She wouldn't dream of standing Wade up. If she didn't show, he would probably have the nerve to come knocking on her front door.

Anne's parents showed up mere moments after Wade's departure. Her father, looking every inch the country squire, wore an official-looking badge that said Judge. He smiled and waved when he caught sight of her, then immediately sobered.

"Your mother says you're not feeling well." His round, jovial face, which disguised a keen intellect that could cut his legal opponents to ribbons, was etched with concern.

"I'm fine. Just tired." She smiled, reassuring him.

"Let's go home and put our feet up," Deborah said, sliding an arm around Anne's waist. "They gave your dad a pie for judging the contest." She pointed to a shopping bag looped over her arm. "We can warm it up and have it with ice cream."

"Don't mention pie," Milton said with a grimace. "I may never eat pie again."

"Oh, that'll be the day," Deborah said.

Anne relaxed slightly as they all climbed into her father's gold Cadillac. Her parents were good people, and they loved her unconditionally. When they pushed her too hard or tried to impose their opinions on her, Anne had to remind herself that everything they did, they did out of love for her. She had come late into their lives—her mother was forty when Anne was born. They had doted on her her whole life, and they only wanted the best for their daughter.

SLIPPING OUT OF THE HOUSE was easy. When her parents were engrossed in TV, Anne tiptoed down the back stairs and out the French doors to the patio, then around to the garage. Their driveway was at the top of a hill, so Anne didn't even have to start her car.

She put her blue Mustang—a graduation present from her father—into Neutral and coasted into the street, breathing a relieved sigh when no one called to her.

The whole escapade felt a little childish, she thought as she started the car's engine half a block away. But the previous few months had upset her parents greatly, and she refused to do anything to cause them more worry.

She knew where the Hardison Ranch was. Even if she hadn't visited there since she was a young girl, everyone knew. It was the biggest cattle operation in Cottonwood, and old Pete Hardison had been one of the town's first residents. Pete had struggled in the early days. Then he'd struck oil and become a millionaire overnight—and adopted the lifestyle to prove it.

The oil bust in the eighties had all but ruined the overextended Hardisons, but Pete's grandson, Jonathan—Wade's oldest brother—had caught the ranching bug. He'd taken hold of the ranch and brought it back to prosperity over the past dozen years.

When Anne pulled up to the Hardison Ranch's white gates, she found them open. She rumbled over the cattle guard and up the red dirt drive, meandering through some mesquite trees before she saw the old barn, looming dark in the night.

She was five minutes late. The barn looked black inside, completely uninhabited, but she sensed Wade was there. She could almost feel him. He didn't seem the type to play games—that was her specialty. If he'd said he'd be here at eleven, he probably was here.

She parked and climbed out of the car. The night

had taken on a slight chill, and the brisk breeze blew up inside her jumper, making her wish she'd put on jeans. She shivered slightly, but more from apprehension than the cold.

The huge double doors of the old-fashioned red barn were slightly ajar, enough that she could squeeze through. "Hello?" she called out as her eyes tried to adjust to the almost total darkness.

She heard the strike of a match, then saw the flare not ten feet in front of her. She could just make out Wade's strong features as he lit a kerosene lantern that looked like an antique. The lantern glowed to life, and Anne could see the cavernous barn was full to the rafters with hay.

"Why were you standing here in the dark?" she asked. "And is it safe to have a lantern in here? All this hay..."

Wade hung the lantern on a hook. "Lots of questions. I like the dark. And the lantern is safe, so long as we don't get so wild we knock it over."

Anne's heart did a flip-flop. If he was trying to unnerve her with his innuendo, he'd succeeded.

Chapter Two

Wade held on to the illusion of confidence like a two-year-old with a security blanket. He tried to pretend Annie showing up here tonight was no big deal. In truth, he'd been terrified she would blow him off.

But Annie had come. She was standing before him, looking like a mirage in the lantern light, her green eyes keeping a wary watch on him. Which meant that maybe she was still interested.

He leaned against a stack of round hay bales and folded his arms. "So, Annie, what's your story? Why the big deception?" he asked, his tone intentionally casual. "And why the disappearing act?" She'd really thrown him for a loop when he'd awakened that Monday morning after the rodeo to find her gone.

He wasn't like a lot of the guys on the circuit who slept with any buckle bunny who came along, making empty promises then awkward goodbyes when it came time to move on to the next rodeo. Not that he was a monk, but he'd thought Annie was special—different.

Worth his time and attention.

Though they'd made no promises, he'd felt so good

when he was with her that he'd been silently plotting ways he could keep her hanging around. He'd thought she felt the same.

She said nothing, just stood there with her hands clenched, staring at the floor.

"Cat got your tongue?" he asked, enjoying her discomfort. "Come on, you're a lawyer. Lawyers have to know how to talk, right? Damn, I never would have guessed."

"The woman you met at the Mesquite Rodeo," she finally said, "that wasn't me. She—"

"I thought we covered that territory earlier."

"I mean, physically she was in my body, but she wasn't the real Anne Chatsworth." She paced, a caged lioness looking for a crack she could squeeze through.

Abruptly she stopped and faced him squarely. Though she still wore the conservative clothes from earlier, some of her hair had worked itself loose from her knot and squiggled around her face. Her eyes were large and luminous, and she'd lost that tight, controlled expression he'd seen at the fair.

"I was studying for finals and having a real hard time," she continued. "The pressure, the doubts, the stress—you can't imagine what that's like unless you go through it."

"You're right, I wouldn't know anything about stress. I'm just a simple cowboy. Is that it?"

"I didn't mean it like that. I'm sure you've had stress in your life at one time or another. I'm just trying to explain where my mind was."

"Okay, I'll agree, you were under pressure. Go on."

"That Friday I kind of lost it. I'd been studying nonstop for hours, days, and I just...snapped. I needed a break. No, I needed more than that. I needed to get away from everything—*forget* everything, including myself."

"Enter Annie the slow-talking rodeo girl."

She looked at him, her face pleading with him to understand.

"I'll be damned," he said. "So I was nothing to you but Cowboy Valium?"

She sank onto a rickety wooden bench. "I guess you could put it that way, although at the beginning I certainly had no intention of...of..."

"...picking up some guy and sleeping with him," he finished for her.

"Exactly."

"But that's what you did. Any particular reason you picked me?"

"You make it sound so premeditated. I recognized your name when the announcer said it. I remembered you, although I'm sure the reverse isn't true. Last time we saw each other, I was twelve and you were sixteen, so I probably didn't register on your radar screen. I used to hang out at the Livestock Exchange arena and watch you practice with Traveler when he was just a colt."

She was right, he'd been focused on other matters. Getting Traveler up to competition speed so he could get the hell out of Cottonwood had been the only thing he could think about back then.

"Anyway, after you won your event, I went back to the chutes to find you so I could say hi, you know, a friendly voice from back home. But I sort of never got around to mentioning Cottonwood.''

''You never even told me your last name. So you could make a clean getaway after you seduced me?''

''Hey, come on. There was a lot of mutual seducing going on, if you'll recall.''

Oh, yeah, he recalled. And so did she, judging from the way she was breathing, quick and shallow, and the flare of heat in her eyes.

''You know, this doesn't sound much like an apology,'' he said.

''I'm getting there. Let me finish.''

''I've got all night.'' He couldn't be sure, because the light was so dim, but he thought she blushed. That was something he loved about redheads, about Annie in particular. It was so easy to make her blush.

''Going to bed with you wasn't a premeditated act. It just happened. And afterward I knew I should go home and forget about it, get on with my studies, but I couldn't make myself leave.''

He remembered that. He remembered how she'd talked about getting home, how he'd actually walked her to her car, but then they'd started kissing again, and she'd forgotten all about leaving. Somehow she'd ended up staying with him all night—then all the next day, then through the weekend.

They hadn't been able to get enough of each other. He'd been crazy about her, unable to think of anything else—even his upcoming rodeo events. Nothing had ever before distracted him from his obsession.

''I guess I needed that time away from my studying more than I knew,'' she said. ''It felt like a drug in my system. The longer I pretended to be Annie, the less I wanted to go back to reality.''

''Did you ever think that maybe Annie *is* your reality? And the other is just an elaborate personality you've invented?''

She looked at him sharply. ''Annie isn't real. I'm not like her. I don't flirt and I don't dress that way. I'm a very serious person who is pursuing a very demanding career. Practicing law has always been my dream, and I'm almost there.''

Well. She'd told him. ''Did you flunk your exams?''

''No. I left you early that Monday morning because I had a test at ten o'clock.''

''You could have woke me up and told me that.''

She shook her head. ''I was afraid you'd talk me into staying. I was really scared by what I'd done, Wade. I panicked. I ran back to the world where I belonged. You and the rodeo—that was a fantasy.''

He stood up, angered by her words, and made a mock bow. ''Glad I could oblige. But next time you need to blow off steam, try racquetball.''

''I didn't think it would matter to you. We both knew it was a temporary thing. You were on the road. I figured you slept with a different girl in every town, that you'd be glad I left without all those uncomfortable goodbyes.''

''Yeah, well, you're right. It stung a little, waking up in that empty bunk, *not even a note,* but it wasn't all that hard to find a replacement.'' Big lie. He hadn't slept with anyone since Annie. Too busy, too focused on the competition. Anyway, every time he looked at an attractive woman now, he compared her to Annie and found her lacking.

Annie had spoiled him.

"That's what I figured." Her voice cracked, making Wade wonder if his barb had found its mark. Did she have any feelings about what happened between them?

"What you did wasn't very nice," he said. "Even if it was just a casual affair."

"I'm sorry I didn't handle the situation better. I was out of my element. I'd never had a one-night stand before."

"Three nights." Three glorious, earth-shattering, life-altering nights of the steamiest lovemaking he'd ever experienced.

"Three nights," she agreed. "It was a wonderful weekend, the best— Oh, hell, I'm going to blow it now."

"I don't think so. Finish what you were saying. My ego could use a boost."

She turned away from him. "It was the best time I ever had."

He came up quietly behind her and put his hands on her shoulders. She tensed, so he didn't push it—didn't press his lips to that sensitive place on her neck he knew about, didn't pull the pins out of that ridiculously tight knot her hair was in, didn't wrap his arms around her body and hold her fast against him until she agreed not to run.

He knew running was exactly what she had in mind, and there was probably nothing he could do about it.

"I guess you're not here to take up where we left off," he said.

"I can't."

"Why not?"

She stepped out of his loose grasp and turned to face him. "A casual affair just isn't my style. Anyway, you wouldn't really want to bother with me. I'm so completely different from Annie."

"Maybe you'd be more like her if you'd smile once in a while. Is that some kind of lifestyle choice?"

"I don't have anything to smile about right now, okay?"

"Your dream coming true doesn't make you smile?"

"It hasn't come true yet. I don't have a job. I haven't passed the bar. Lots of hurdles to jump."

"So you're under a lot of stress."

"Yes. Exactly."

He ran one finger down her cheek, gratified to feel her tremble. Nice to know he still had some effect on her. "I know a really good stress buster. It's called Cowboy Valium."

She hesitated a fraction of a second longer, then jumped out of his reach. "No. That's not why I came here. And if you chose this isolated place for us to meet so you could seduce me, you're in for a disappointment."

"As I recall, lady, you were the one who insisted on privacy."

"It would be pointless to start something. I'll be leaving town again in a couple of weeks. And I can't afford any distractions. I've got job interviews, I've got to study for the bar..."

"Who are you trying to convince?"

"I'm just not the temporary-fling type."

Neither was he. But unlike Anne, he wasn't convinced a fling was all they could have. Sure, the circumstances worked against them, but anything was possible if they put their minds to it.

If he spoke his thoughts out loud, she would probably break something running away from him. A skittish woman like Anne required careful handling.

The kindest thing he could do right now was let her go. Unfortunately, he wasn't feeling kind. "You can't tell me you're not real, Annie."

"Stop calling me Annie."

"The woman called Annie is part of you. You can't convince me otherwise. And if you ask me, Annie is worth a dozen uptight, frowning, defeminized, frumpish Anne Chatsworths. A fat paycheck and a sixty-hour workweek won't keep you warm at night, and it won't make you laugh, and it'll probably send you to an early grave. Stress does that, you know."

She was silent, and Wade was afraid he'd gone too far. So much for careful handling.

She turned and stalked out of the barn, and Wade didn't follow her. Moments later he heard her car starting, then tires spinning in dirt as she peeled out.

ANNE FUMED the whole way home. She was so mad, in fact, that she forgot to be quiet when she pulled her car into the driveway. She got out and slammed the door, then made all kinds of noise as she entered the same way she'd come out.

Uptight, frowning, defeminized, frumpish… Just because she wasn't wearing tight jeans and a low-cut blouse? Because she hadn't troweled on two pounds of makeup, and her hair wasn't teased up Dolly Parton big?

How dare Wade Hardison try to tell her how to live her life? Just because she'd spent a weekend with him, did that make him think he knew everything about her?

She was furious that he made her so tongue-tied, really ticked that he'd gotten in the last word. What kind of lawyer would she be if she froze up when an opponent got the advantage? She'd completely lost her cool. And, damn it, her cool was one of the few things she had going for her right now.

"Anne?"

Anne stopped short as she entered the kitchen. Her father was making himself a cup of hot cocoa. "Oh, hi, Dad." *Stay calm, don't let him see that anything's wrong.* He would only worry about her.

"Where have you been?" he asked with a frown. "I thought you'd gone to bed."

"I couldn't sleep, so I went for a drive."

"Why didn't you let us know you were leaving?"

"C'mon, Dad, I'm not sixteen anymore."

"I know, honey, but we're still allowed to worry about you, aren't we? If your mother had stopped in your room to say good-night, she would have been frantic to find you gone."

Anne sighed. "You're right. I'm sorry. I'll be more considerate in the future."

Milton smiled. "Want some hot chocolate? Might help you sleep."

"No, thanks. I'm tired now. Good night." She kissed her father on the cheek, then slipped up the back stairs, avoiding her mother and the inevitable questions. She'd probably still get them at breakfast tomorrow, but she'd be in better shape to answer them after a good night's sleep.

If she could get one. She was still steamed, and her blood felt hot in her veins—not just from anger, but desire. She still wanted Wade Hardison's body with the same intensity she'd experienced at the rodeo, despite everything that had happened. She could still feel the warm pressure of his hands on her shoulders, the tickle of his breath against her neck. Though she would never admit it, it had taken all of her willpower to turn down Wade's suggestion that they take up where they'd left off.

She would just have to avoid him for however long he was in town. Which reminded her—how long *was* he in town? Why was he here, when he'd sworn to her he would never go home, never be forgiven by his family? What had changed his mind?

ON HIS WAY BACK to the house, Wade stopped in the new, modern barn his brother Jonathan had built. He wanted to check on Traveler. The bay quarter horse stood in his stall, completely still, probably asleep. Normally Traveler was alert the moment anyone came near him. His inertia concerned Wade almost as much as the injury. Maybe it was the medicine.

Wade resisted the urge to scratch the stallion's forelock, Traveler's favorite form of affection. The horse might need to sleep.

He started to turn away, then heard a familiar

nicker. He turned and smiled. Traveler must have caught his scent and wakened. Wade scratched the horse's black forelock, like he'd wanted to do, then behind his ears, then rubbed the soft skin under his jaw. Traveler nuzzled Wade's ear, then searched his hands for a treat.

"Sorry, buddy, I gave you the last carrot after dinner." Traveler made a pleading noise, and Wade, as usual, caved in. "Oh, all right. But too many treats while you can't exercise, and you'll get fat." He found a handful of oats and fed it to the horse, grateful that at least Traveler had rediscovered his appetite. For a couple of days after his injury, when he'd been in pain and pumped up with drugs, he'd wanted nothing to do with food.

Wade changed the compress on Traveler's right front leg, then spent a few minutes grooming him, even though he didn't need it. Still, he knew the horse enjoyed the attention. Traveler had always loved to have Wade curry him. He even stood still while Wade worked a tangle out of his tail.

That done, Wade gave the stallion a few parting pats, then headed back to the house. It was after midnight. He doubted anyone would be up to question what he was doing out so late.

As he poured himself a glass of milk, he thought again about the woman who called herself Anne Chatsworth. He actually liked her more serious side, despite what he'd said. Life wasn't all fun and games, as it had been for Annie.

Anne was very different from the flirtatious, easygoing country girl who'd wooed him at the rodeo in Dallas—and yet he saw flashes of Annie rippling to the surface every now and then. Annie wasn't some fictitious character, she was a very real part of Anne that had somehow been vanquished.

By whom or what? he wondered. And when?

It was fine for a woman to want a career. He knew what it was like to be focused on a goal, to think about it night and day, to dream about reaching the top. Lord knew he'd spent a good deal of his life in that very state. Sure, there were frustrations along the way. Stress. Setbacks. Doubts. But his rodeo work had always brought him joy. His eyes were always on the goal, but he hadn't been so obsessed that he hadn't enjoyed the journey.

Joy seemed to be missing from Anne's life. She was on the verge of embarking on the path she'd been preparing for all these years, yet he sensed no anticipation, no excitement. She probably had her pick of law firms. She could go to any city she wanted, explore all kinds of different career possibilities. Yet all he sensed in her was sorrow.

Maybe it was none of his business, but he couldn't leave it at that. He'd seen what happened to people who weren't living a life that made them happy. His mother was the perfect example. She'd been brilliant—could have been a Nobel prize-winning scientist. But she'd met Wade's father at some medical conference and had opted for the life of a small-town doctor's wife.

The lack of intellectual stimulation had ultimately killed her. Oh, technically it was cancer, but Wade had recognized that she'd lost the will to live.

One of the last things she'd told him was that he had to follow his dream, even if it wasn't the same dream his family wanted for him. He'd held those words close to his heart, followed her advice and never regretted it.

What he did regret was the way he'd left Cottonwood—angry, bitter, full of the bullheaded pride only a teenage boy can exhibit. Too damn proud to apologize for things he never should have said. He regretted the family rift, one he could have healed a long time ago if he'd tried.

To Wade's surprise he found his brother Jonathan in the den watching TV. Jonathan was a rancher down to his marrow, which meant early mornings. He was seldom up past nine o'clock in the evening.

Wade considered sneaking on up to bed, then decided he might be passing up an opportunity. It was hard to talk to Jonathan because he was always so busy. The man hardly ever stood still.

Wade stepped into the den and without a word plopped down on the couch and propped his booted feet on the coffee table. If Jonathan was in the mood to talk, he'd say something. If not, well, a few minutes of companionable silence wouldn't hurt.

Jonathan was watching an old John Wayne movie. Typical. Wade wasn't a big fan of the Duke, but he watched, anyway.

"Where you been?" Jonathan finally asked.

"With Traveler."

"He doin' any better?"

"Swelling's down. Doc Chandler says we can start physical therapy tomorrow."

"Good. If anyone can get your old horse back in top form, Chandler can."

"He's not old."

"He's thirteen."

"Lots of horses compete well into their teens."

A long pause. Then Jonathan asked, "Seen the new filly Larry's been training?"

"The black? Yeah, nice-looking animal."

"Rodeo potential?"

Strange question, coming from Jonathan, who'd never made it a secret he thought rodeo was the biggest waste of time and livestock on earth.

"Spirited," Wade replied. "Lots of explosive power, probably be fast out of a chute. Good heart, seems eager to please."

"But?"

"Easily distracted. Shies at anything."

"She's still young. She might get over that."

"With the right training," Wade agreed.

Another pause. "You want to work with her?"

Wade's heart leaped at the chance to train such a fine-looking horse. If he could turn a mutt like Traveler into a champion, just imagine what he could do with— He stopped his runaway imagination, spotting the trap.

"Ah, no, no thanks. I start working your stock, next thing you know I'll be out castrating calves."

Jonathan abruptly shut off the television, silencing the Duke midsentence. "You ungrateful little—"

"What? Just because I don't want to work as an unpaid ranch hand? Why do you think I left here in the first place?"

"If you'd listen once in a while instead of jumping to conclusions, you might not be such a hothead."

"Hothead?"

"I thought if you worked with the mare, and you

liked her, I might give her to you. I was not plotting to turn you into slave labor.''

Well, that took the wind right out of Wade's sails.

''You might say thanks.''

''Yeah, thanks.'' Amazing how hard that one word was to push past his teeth. ''I don't need two horses, though.''

''Traveler's competition days might be over.''

Wade's jaw tensed, and he consciously relaxed it. ''He'll be fine.''

Jonathan shrugged. ''This time, maybe. But what about next year?''

''I'll worry about that when the time comes.'' And maybe, just maybe, he wouldn't have to worry about it.

''So where were you, really?'' Jonathan asked. ''I was at the barn till eleven-thirty. You weren't with Traveler.''

''It's been a lot of years since anybody kept tabs on my activities.''

''Just curious.''

''I was with a woman.''

Jonathan looked his younger brother up and down. ''You work fast. You've been here, what, three days?''

''We were just talking.''

''Who? Or am I being too nosy?''

''Too nosy.'' He wasn't ready to talk about his Annie to anyone yet. Especially not when she'd just shot him down so thoroughly.

He wasn't done with her, though. She might not know it yet, but she needed him, and not just for a weekend. Somebody had to put a smile back on that girl's face—and keep it there.

Chapter Three

"Well, Anne, everything looks great," Jeff Hardison said, closing the folder that held her chart. "Your weight's almost back to normal, there's no sign of infection, and you've even smiled at me once or twice."

She appreciated his vote of confidence. Jeff had seen her at her worst, and it was partly due to his conscientious care that she was looking and feeling so much better. Not back to normal. She'd been broken and glued back together—she probably would never be exactly the same person she was before. But at least she was in one piece and moving forward.

"I'm feeling great," she confirmed. "So why do we have to do the blood tests?"

"Anne, we've been over this."

"But I'm not sure there's really a point. I'd like to move forward, not dwell on the past."

"This *is* looking forward," he insisted. "If there's a problem, it could affect your ability to have children in the future."

"I don't plan to have children."

"You might change your mind. You're only twenty-five."

He had a point. For the next five to ten years she would not have the time to devote to raising a family. Her law career would demand 100 percent of her concentration. If she had a husband, kids, they would only end up neglected—and what was the point in that?

But once she was established, once she'd paid her dues, she might want to switch gears. She wasn't dumb enough to believe a career could answer all of her needs.

"All right. Might as well get it over with."

"I'll have Molly draw the blood. She's so gentle, it'll feel like a butterfly kiss."

"Yeah, right." Anne laughed despite her concerns.

"It's good to hear you laugh. Keep it up, huh?"

In a treatment room a few minutes later, Anne determinedly studied a spot on the wall while Molly, Jeff's nurse, deftly inserted a needle into Anne's arm. As long as she didn't look at the needle or see the blood, she would be okay. At least, that was what she told herself.

She'd put off her follow-up visit to Jeff for several days, until Jeff himself had called the house and reminded her. Even knowing he wanted her blood, she hadn't been able to come up with a graceful excuse. So here she was, letting Molly torture her.

"They're having a sale over at Hollywood Lingerie," Molly said, continuing her nonstop monologue. Anne didn't know if Molly's chatter was designed to distract patients from the procedure or if she just liked to talk, but it did help.

"I've never been there," Anne made herself answer. "What kind of stuff do they have? Ouch."

"Sorry. Well, a lot of real naughty stuff, that's what. Negligees with cutouts in places you just can't believe, and panties so sheer you might as well not be wearing any."

Anne didn't own any sexy lingerie. She'd been raised in practical white cotton, which her mother insisted was the only sort of underwear a real lady would wear. In college she'd branched out to pastels, but that was as wild as she'd gotten.

She'd never thought much about it until her weekend with Wade. She'd been wearing all those provocative outer clothes, which Wade had taken a great deal of pleasure in removing. But then came her underwear—they were so dull! They didn't fit the Annie image at all.

"My Tom can be the most boring man in the world," Molly went on, "but show him a pair of black lace panties and he turns into Casanova."

"So you actually wear that stuff?"

"Honey, nothing makes you feel sexier. And I'm telling you, men can sense it when you're wearing a hot-pink teddy, even if you have all your clothes on. Sexy underwear gives you an attitude."

"Maybe I'll stop by and take a look." Her mother would have a conniption if she found hot-pink anything in the laundry. Then again, Deborah didn't do the laundry—she had a housekeeper for that.

Ordinarily Anne wouldn't worry so much about upsetting her parents. But the past couple of months had shaken both of them to their foundations. She had promised herself she would make it up to them by being their ideal daughter, at least while she was living under their roof.

"All done," Molly said, pressing a cotton ball to the inside of Anne's arm, then folding the arm to hold the cotton tight against her traumatized vein. "That wasn't so bad."

"Not for you," Anne quipped.

"Dr. Jeff wants to see you again before you leave. Let me see if I can catch him between patients, and I'll send him in. Now, you just drink that orange juice and rest."

Molly left with a whole trayful of blood-filled test tubes. The sight of all that red made Anne lightheaded, so she was happy to sit still for a few minutes and recover from the ordeal. She wondered why Jeff wanted to see her again. Hadn't they covered all the territory?

Almost immediately someone tapped discreetly on the treatment-room door.

"Come in," Anne called.

Jeff entered, looking tall and reassuring in his white coat. "I see you survived. A butterfly kiss, was I right?"

"Molly is a charming little vampire. Was there something else?"

"I'm heading next door for coffee. You want to come?"

"Sure, I could use a coffee."

Jeff took off his white coat, stashed it in his office, then led Anne past the receptionist with a wave. "Back in a few."

They walked next door to a little take-out café that served coffee and bagels and not much else. With cappuccinos in hand, they settled at a little table in the corner.

"Your mother tells me you haven't been getting out much," Jeff mentioned casually.

"Mmm, too busy." She took a sip of the rich coffee drink. Heaven.

"You know that's not healthy, right? I'm asking as a friend, not your doctor. Physically you're recovering nicely, but I'm a little worried about your mood."

"Oh, Jeff, don't be silly. I'm okay. You heard me laugh a few minutes ago, remember?"

"I'm serious. I know you've been hurt recently, and it takes time to get over that. But I don't want you to dwell on it."

Jeff assumed she'd been dumped by the baby's father, and she hadn't set him straight. He had no idea she and Wade even knew each other outside their brief, childhood acquaintance—and she wanted to keep it that way.

"The best tonic for a broken heart," he continued, "is to just get right back out there, you know, come up swinging. It's like falling off a horse. You want to get right back on before you build the fear up in your head so much that you can never—"

"Jeff, what are you saying?"

"I'm saying, why don't we go to a movie or something?"

"You're kidding." Realizing how rude she sounded, she quickly backpedaled. "I mean, oh, Jeff, that's really sweet. I'm so flattered, I mean..." What did she mean? This was so weird, so unexpected. Jeff was considered the town catch. Every single woman in town had made a play for him at one time or another. Why would he make a play for her, the town brain? She'd never been anything to him except a little sister—and a patient.

"You can change to being Dad's patient, if you're uneasy about dating your doctor," he said, as if reading her mind. "Dad would welcome you back."

"I'm not ready to date," she said, in no uncertain terms. "Anyway, I'm so busy..." Oh, did that sound lame. "In a few weeks I'll be taking a job in another city. It wouldn't make sense for us to...start anything."

He flashed her his most winning smile. "I'm talking about dinner and a movie, not some great love affair."

At some other time in her life, she might be tempted. Jeff was movie-star handsome, charming and a good friend. But not now. She just couldn't wrap her mind around dating, even a casual evening.

"Oookay, I get the picture," he said when she didn't respond. "How 'bout them Cowboys, huh?" He drained his coffee in one gulp, then flashed a grin, letting her know she hadn't wounded him too seriously.

"I appreciate your concern, I really do. And if my parents start driving me crazy, maybe I'll call you and we can go to a movie."

He nodded, seeming to understand. "Deal."

She stood up, grabbed her purse.

"I'll call when we get the test results back," he said, as if their previous conversation had never happened. "It could take a while."

"Okay, no problem." She headed for the café door, in desperate need of fresh air. "Bye, now."

But a hasty escape wasn't in the cards. As she exited, she ran smack into Edward, Jeff and Wade's father.

"Whoa, there, what's your hurry?" he said with a laugh, steadying Anne.

She'd always adored Edward Hardison, or Dr. Ed, as most people called him. With his silver hair and his round, jovial face, he'd always seemed very safe to her, a safe person to take care of her health. But when she'd realized she was pregnant, she'd deliberately made an appointment with Jeff, not his father. The idea of kindly Dr. Ed knowing such a dark secret about her hadn't seemed right. It would have been like telling her father all over again.

Of course, in the end, Edward had found out. As luck would have it, he was taking calls for Jeff when Anne had lost the baby. He'd been just as kind and sympathetic as Jeff, in no way judgmental.

She murmured a greeting, then something about having an appointment, and got out of there, Jeff's invitation still burning in her brain.

She felt badly that she hadn't handled things better. Fending off handsome men wasn't exactly her forte. In fact, she'd seldom had to fend off men at all, handsome or not. Now, in the span of just a few days, she'd turned down two.

She wasn't terribly pretty. She'd learned that lesson well in her teenage years. Skinny, freckled redheads weren't the stuff of any man's dreams. She'd compensated by being the class brain, the one with the quick wit and the acid tongue. She'd played down her femininity, believing her intelligence would take her a lot further than batting her eyelashes and showing cleavage.

That was before Annie. When she'd adopted her alter ego, she'd tapped into a well of femininity she hadn't known existed. And though after her weekend with Wade she'd gone back to her conservative clothes and no-nonsense manner, maybe, just maybe, some essence of Annie remained.

Why else would Jeff suddenly take an interest, even a casual one, in her?

The idea that Annie might be peeking through Anne's hard-fought control both thrilled and frightened her.

She didn't feel like going home, even though she had a stack of applications to fill out and a list of follow-up phone calls to make. Her father had helped her put together an exhaustive list of every large, prestigious law firm in the country. A few of them had already approached her, but Milton had insisted she leave no stone unturned. He didn't want her to miss her golden opportunity simply because she hadn't been thorough enough.

He'd also encouraged her not to jump to any decisions.

Anne had followed his advice to the letter. Right after graduating, she'd gone on several interviews with the firms who had courted her. Despite a few very attractive offers, she'd put them all on ice while she explored other possible options.

Then she'd found out she was pregnant, and all bets were off.

Predictably, her mother had cried and her father had ranted and raved. Anne had simply become paralyzed. The life of an associate in a huge law firm was not compatible with single motherhood. She would end up shortchanging both her employer and her child—and there was never any question about her keeping the child. She'd put all her career plans on hold and focused on preparing for a baby.

She had tried halfheartedly to locate Wade, figuring he had a right to know. But at that time he'd been moving around so much he was impossible to pin down. She'd left a message here and there, but if he'd gotten them, he hadn't responded.

Then she'd lost the baby, and her whole world had turned inside out—again. She hadn't thought it possible to love a child so much when she hadn't even met it. Having the baby ripped from her so cruelly had left her crushed and aching, physically and emotionally.

She'd seen no point in sharing that pain with Wade. She still didn't.

Now, one month after the miscarriage, she was pouring herself into the job search once again. Milton was smiling again. Her world felt a bit more sane. And she knew that soon she would regain the sense of anticipation she'd always had about carving out her own name in the big bad world of lawyers.

Still, the prospect of job hunting seemed decidedly unattractive on a beautiful, Indian Summer day like today. Instead she drove to Hollywood Lingerie and bought two bra-and-panty sets, a black silk camisole and tap pants, and a slinky, midnight-blue nightgown.

A huge garden center was just down the way from Hollywood Lingerie, which inspired Anne to think about a fall garden. Her mother had been talking about pansies and impatiens, and the store beckoned with flats and flats of those very flowers.

Anne took her time picking out the colors, mentally designing the flower beds in front of the house.

"If I'd known all it took was some flowers to make you smile, I'd have got you a truckload."

"Wade?" Oh, for heaven's sake, what was Wade Hardison doing at a garden center? But here he was, big as life, standing in front of her, smiling in that lazy, easy way of his, as if they ran into each other on the street every day.

Even more surprising were Wade's companions, a little boy about seven and a girl, maybe four or five. She recognized them as Sam and Kristin, Jonathan Hardison's two kids.

Putting aside her lingering pique over her and Wade's last meeting, she smiled at both children. "Who do we have here? Don't tell me that's Sam and Kristin. They're too big to be Sam and Kristin."

The little girl hid her face against Wade's jean-clad leg.

Anne's heart fluttered dangerously. Lately she couldn't look at a child without thinking of the one she lost, but right now she couldn't afford to be maudlin. She ruthlessly pushed aside the thought of her own baby.

"C'mon, you guys remember me, right?" Anne cajoled. "I was at your house on the Fourth of July. I'm Anne."

"Kids, say hi to Annie," Wade prompted.

Anne gave him a sharp look.

"Uh, Anne. Her name's Anne."

"I 'member you, Anne. We're making a terrarium

for our frogs,'' Sam said proudly, pulling a jar from their shopping cart, which also held several small green plants and some decorative rocks. He extended the jar for Anne's inspection. Inside the jar, which contained a little moist dirt, were two of the tiniest frogs she had ever seen, no bigger than the end of her finger.

''Oh, aren't they cute,'' she said, taking the jar and holding it up to the light. ''I had a pet frog once.''

''We caught 'em as tadpoles,'' Sam said, ''and they took all summer to grow legs. Now they need a better home.''

''Do these frogs have names?'' Anne asked.

''Mine's Alexander the Great,'' Sam said.

''And mine's Miss Pooh Bear,'' Kristin piped in, apparently having overcome her shyness. ''Do you have a boo-boo?'' She pointed to the Band-Aid on Anne's inner arm.

''Just a little one. Thank you for asking, Kristin.''

Wade wasn't satisfied with her answer. ''I haven't noticed the Bloodmobile around town.''

''Ah, no, I have your brother to blame for this.''

Wade rolled his eyes. ''Jeff and his needles. You're not sick, are you?''

Anne waved away his concern, hoping she did a good job of sounding nonchalant. ''No, of course not. Just a routine blood test.''

''What for?''

''Nosy, aren't we? Jeff is checking to see whether I have two X chromosomes,'' she answered without missing a beat. ''You know, since I'm so—'' she lowered her voice ''—defeminized.''

"Oh, come on, Anne, don't hold that against me. It was a moment of desperation."

"Of course I'm holding it against you. What else would you expect from an uptight, frowning—"

"Okay, okay, I get the point. I'm sorry. I was way out of line. You don't look at all defeminized today."

She felt idiotically pleased by the compliment. She was just wearing a pair of jeans and short-sleeved cashmere sweater, but it had to look better on her than that potato-sack jumper she'd worn to Autumn Daze. She turned away and pretended interest in a potting-soil display.

"Looks like you're planning quite a gardening project," Wade said.

"They're for my mother."

"Hey, what's in there?" Kristin asked, pointing to Anne's shopping cart. To her mortification, the child was pointing to her Hollywood Lingerie bag, which was pink and sparkly and naturally attractive to a five-year-old girl.

"Yeah, I'd like to know that, too," Wade said with a wink.

Busted. Why hadn't she put the bag in her trunk before shopping for flowers? Didn't she know what kind of speculation she might invite, carrying around a bag like that?

"Socks," she finally said, her voice coming out sounding strangled. "They were on sale."

She could tell Wade didn't believe her, and she hoped the rush of heated blood through her veins didn't reveal itself in a blush. He would have to pry that bag out of her cold dead hands before she would admit what was in there.

"I've really got to get home," she said, turning her basket toward the checkout lanes.

"No time to chat with an old friend?" His voice was like warm honey—not his normal voice, which was pleasant enough, deep and smooth and sort of musical, but the voice he used in seduction mode.

Their gazes locked, and the store background noises receded, replaced by the roar of Anne's blood in her ears. She could kiss him right here, right in the middle of Garden City. What was wrong with her? Why did all her powers of discretion and common sense disintegrate around Wade?

He ran one finger up her arm, which answered her question. She cast a nervous glance at the kids, but their attention had been captured by a giant plastic ant guarding a display of insecticides.

Did she just imagine the way his eyes seemed to change from ordinary brown to dark chocolate when he looked at her? Maybe she was reading way more into his gesture than he intended.

She took one step back. "Cut it out, Wade."

"No one's looking at us."

"Can I be any clearer? I do not want to—" She realized both children had turned and were staring at her, fascinated with whatever she was about to say.

"Careful," Wade said. "Little pitchers..."

"You know what I don't want."

"I know what you do want. And you want it bad."

Anne was sure her face was bright pink as she took her turn with the cashier. The worst part of it was, he was right. She *did* want it. But all of her objections to renewing her relationship with Wade still held firm. He'd been perfect for slam-bam Annie, but the real

Anne was more fragile. She didn't want to be hurt. Besides, he'd be gone soon and so would she.

She quickly paid for her flowers, said a hasty good-bye to the children, pointedly ignored Wade and made her escape.

Under some other circumstances, perhaps, she would take Wade up on his offer. She liked him, liked him more each time she saw him, even when he played cat and mouse with her. She liked how devoted he was to his horse—he treated Traveler more like a pampered lapdog than working livestock. She was surprised by his ease with the children. They were perfectly comfortable with him, and he obviously had a soft spot for them.

Just as his initial impressions of her were wrong, maybe he wasn't the one-dimensional rodeo Romeo she'd pegged him as.

Well, it was a moot point now.

When Anne arrived home, Deborah was thrilled to see the flowers. ''I've completely neglected the yard for months,'' she said as she helped unload the Mustang's trunk, and Anne felt a little twinge of guilt. The only reason her mother had neglected anything was because she'd focused her entire existence on Anne and her dilemma. ''These are perfect. Will you help me plant them?''

''She's got work to do,'' Milton interjected.

''But, Milton,'' Deborah objected, ''she needs to get more fresh air and sunshine.''

''She'll get plenty of that tomorrow.''

''What's tomorrow?'' Anne wanted to know.

''A barbecue—at the Hardisons'. It's for Pete's eightieth birthday. Don't tell me I forgot to tell you.''

"Yes, you did. I don't think I can make it," Anne said automatically. The last people she wanted to be around were the Hardisons, particularly Jeff or Wade.

"But you have to, dear. Pete Hardison hasn't seen you since last Christmas, and you know you're one of his favorites. His feelings would be hurt if you skipped his birthday party."

Deborah was right. "Grandpa Pete," as she called him, had doted on her when her family had first moved to Cottonwood. He'd never had a daughter or granddaughter of his own, so he'd informally adopted Anne.

"Will the whole family be there?" Anne asked.

"I assume so. Even Wade. I don't know if you heard or not, but he's back home."

Anne jumped, but as her mother grabbed a flat of plants and set them on the garage floor, she seemed to assign no particular significance to dropping Wade's name.

"You remember him, don't you?" Deborah carried on chattily. "He ran away when he was sixteen, ran off and joined the circus or something. You were just a little girl. Anyway, he's come back, the proverbial prodigal son."

"Yes, I remember him." In far too much detail.

Deborah turned back to Anne. "How was your checkup, anyway?"

"Fine." She hadn't told her parents about the blood tests. It wasn't something they needed to know at this stage in their lives. With any luck, they'd never have to know.

"Anne, what's this?" Deborah held up a tiny, green plastic pot with a sprig of ivy. One of the Hardison clan's terrarium plants had apparently migrated into her cart.

Anne shrugged. "An impulse purchase." Once again, she felt her traitorous face heating.

"I've got at least a dozen ivy plants rooting in the sunroom."

Anne forced a smile. "I said it was an impulse. I didn't say it was smart."

ANNE MANAGED to put Wade out of her mind for most of the rest of the day by keeping really busy. That night, after all the gardening and phone calls and applications, she was so exhausted she fell immediately into a deep, dreamless sleep.

At precisely 3:00 a.m. she sat bolt-upright in bed with the most disturbing thoughts. Wade and those kids...

When she'd found out she was pregnant, she'd thought a lot about how she would break the news to Wade. In her imaginings, the conversation was always hideous:

"Wade, I don't know how this happened, but I'm going to have your baby."

"No way. That's impossible. We were careful."

"Not careful enough, apparently. There was that first time..."

"How do you know it's mine?"

"Because you're the only guy I've slept with in the past year."

"Like I believe that."

"I don't want anything from you. I just thought you should know."

"Yeah, well, you've done your civic duty." Click.

She had no real reason to believe he would treat her like that, but she hadn't had any trouble imagining how a guy like Wade would feel about fatherhood. Nightmare city. He didn't even have a permanent address, owned nothing but his horse, truck, trailer and the clothes on his back. Obviously, he had no desire to be tied down.

After she'd lost the baby, her mother had tried to comfort her by saying the miscarriage was probably for the best, that a child should grow up with two parents. Anne had forced herself to agree, outwardly at least, to keep the peace. She'd even allowed herself some degree of relief because now she wouldn't have to track down Wade and tell him he was going to be a father.

But that was before she'd seen him with Sam and Kristin. He was good with them. He obviously thought they hung the stars. Maybe he even fantasized about having kids of his own one day. And they adored him. Contrary to all her preconceived ideas, Wade Hardison might make a pretty good father.

And she'd lost his baby.

Anne was ashamed she hadn't even given him a chance to prove what kind of father he could be. But now it was too late.

Chapter Four

"The swelling's gone down a lot," Dr. Rick Chandler pronounced as he poked and prodded at Traveler's leg.

"He's feeling better, too," Wade said. "I can tell he's itching to get out of this stall."

"Then let's give it a try."

Full of optimism, Wade attached a lead rope to Traveler's halter, then opened the stall door and let all three of them out. To his disappointment, his horse put almost no weight on the injured leg, gimping along with an awkward gait. They walked the length of the barn, then back, with the vet observing critically. When they reached Traveler's stall the horse entered docilely, then didn't even turn around to face front—as if his infirmity humiliated him.

Doc Chandler frowned. "He's still in a lot of pain."

"Should I continue the hot and cold compresses?"

"Couldn't hurt, at least until the swelling's gone. Don't let him walk around on that leg just yet."

"You think there's any way he'll be ready for the American Royal in early November?"

The vet scratched his grizzled white head. He'd been treating Cottonwood's animal population since long before Wade was born, and he seemed to have a special bond with animals. In fact, he'd been in attendance when Traveler was born.

"It's a tough call. Older horses take longer to recover from injuries, just like old people—you know that. And I sure as hell wouldn't push him before he's ready."

"No, I wouldn't do that. But the Royal..."

"You're up for some big prize money, aren't you?"

"The whole enchilada. Even with taking off this whole month, I've still got more points than any other calf roper in the country. I could walk away with enough to retire."

Doc raised his eyebrows.

"I'm not talking a villa on the Riviera, but I'd have enough of a nest egg I could do something else."

"Rodeo getting a little old?"

Wade laughed. "Not hardly. I love rodeo. It's just that I'm not getting any younger. And it's a young man's game. I just have this feeling in my bones, you know, like I'm gonna win the championship this year or I can forget it."

The older man stared at Wade for a few moments, and Wade got the feeling he understood. Doc Chandler had been a bull rider once upon a time, or so Wade had heard.

"I'll do what I can for your horse. These soft-tissue injuries are tricky. They can linger for months, or they can suddenly get better."

"I'm pulling for the 'suddenly better' option."

Wade got out his wallet to pay Doc Chandler's fee, but the vet waved away the cash. "It's just a follow-up visit. No charge. Besides, I'm getting ready to go up to the house and eat my weight in barbecued beef. That's payment enough."

"Thanks." Wade suspected Doc was going easy on him, and he was grateful. He wasn't poor—he'd socked away a good bit of money over the years. But he had a goal in mind. He wouldn't retire until he'd reached it, and every penny he saved moved his bank balance that much closer to his goal.

He'd never told anyone about his pie-in-the-sky plan of raising quarter horses, or the other, even sillier-sounding plan—more a dream than anything. He'd never heard of anyone running a rodeo camp for city kids. But he knew in his gut the camp could work.

Recently he'd started to think about his dreams in more concrete terms—how to get sponsors and grants to help underwrite the project, how to market the camp. He'd started drafting letters, crunching numbers, making calls to the Small Business Association. It was becoming less a dream and more a possibility.

His brothers would laugh their butts off if he told them what he wanted to do with his life. They had him pegged as the ne'er-do-well, the black-sheep brother, who by some fluke had achieved a measure of success in what they considered a worthless field—rodeo. They still didn't consider riding a horse for entertainment a proper career. His oldest brother had never forgiven him for not staying to work the ranch. His father and Jeff, both nonranchers, were at least a bit more sympathetic when it came to Wade following his own path. But they'd never forgiven him for skipping out on that education thing.

"You're sticking around for the big wingding, aren't you?" Doc Chandler asked as he stepped into the barn's bathroom to wash his hands, then comb his hair and his handlebar mustache.

"Command performance. Granddad really would disown me if I skipped out on his eightieth birthday."

"I expect you won't have such a terrible time," Doc teased. "The Hardisons have always known how to throw a party."

Wade wasn't big on parties, but he wouldn't miss this one even without the threat of familial disapproval. The Chatsworths were on the guest list, and that meant Anne was invited, too. He was curious to see whether she would show up and, if she did, how she would treat him in front of their respective relatives. Would she pretend she barely knew him?

That thought cut him to the quick.

He washed his own hands, retucked his shirt into his jeans, then headed up to the house with Doc. Cars and pickups were already arriving, lining the long, red dirt driveway.

The whole family was gathered in the living room—Jeff and his date du jour, Allison, Jonathan and the two kids, Wade's father and Pete, seated in a high-back rocking chair like a king on his throne, allowing the arriving guests to pay him homage. A growing pile of cards and presents—most of them appearing to be bottles of liquor—sat near his feet.

Also there to help with the food was their neighbor, Sally Enderlin, an elderly widow who'd lived in Cottonwood almost as long as Pete. She'd pitched in to help after Wade's mother had died and had become almost part of their family.

As Doc entered the living room, everyone greeted him warmly. Then they all seemed to stare at Wade, unsure how to react. Pete's smile faded, replaced by a disapproving frown. That seemed to be about all Wade could get out of his grandfather.

"'Bout time you showed up," Pete said.

"Oh, leave the boy alone, you old coot," Doc said, coming to Wade's defense. He was one of the few senior citizens in the room who had earned the right to talk to Pete like that. "We were checking on Traveler."

"Don't know why you're bothering," Pete said. "Horse goes lame like that, he's no better'n glue."

Pete was trying to get a rise out of his errant grandson, and Wade refused to give him the satisfaction.

"Wade, well if my eyes don't deceive me, it *is* you," Sally said, wrapping her ropy arms around him. He hugged her back, suddenly feeling loved for the first time in a while. "You'll have to catch me up on your life when you have—oh, here, now, have you met Allison?"

Always the social chairperson, Sally made quick introductions, then flitted away to take a newcomer's coat. Wade was glad Sally was there to play hostess. Certainly none of the Hardison men were very good at that kind of thing.

Wade remembered Allison Crane. She and Jeff had been best friends all through school, though Wade had always suspected that Allison wished she and Jeff could be something more.

"You've changed," Allison said.

"So have you," Wade countered, though in reality, she looked much the same as she had in high school, chubby and plain, but with a beautiful smile. "I hear you're a dentist now."

She nodded, then narrowed her eyes. "Do you wear a mouth guard when you ride?"

"Yes, ma'am."

But she wasn't giving him her full attention. Her eyes kept flickering toward Jeff, keeping tabs on his movements. Same old Allison, same unrequited crush.

As more and more guests arrived, the crowd spilled through the house and outside to the patio, where a deejay played country songs and a couple of the ranch hands were roasting beef, pork and chicken over a pit barbecue. The din of voices got louder and louder as the guests imbibed. Still, Wade knew exactly when Anne arrived. He picked her voice out over the roar the moment she opened her mouth.

Pete actually smiled when he saw Anne. He pushed himself out of his chair despite her protests and kissed her on the cheek. Wade, watching from the doorway to the kitchen, was surprised by the warm greeting. He vaguely remembered his grandfather doting on Anne when she was a little girl, claiming she was his honorary granddaughter, but he hadn't realized they were still close.

"Food and drink's out back," Pete said, pointing toward the kitchen. "Wade, make yourself useful for once and show the Chatsworths where the grub is."

Wade's gaze locked with Anne's. She wore loose khaki slacks and a bulky sweater, her hair pulled back into a single braid. The sexless clothes and unimaginative hairstyle didn't really bother him as much as he let on. He knew what she looked like underneath. In fact, he could almost sense the Annie he remembered from the rodeo seething beneath the surface, ready to leap out.

Despite what she said, Annie was not fictional.

Anne's father seemed to be waiting for some introduction, so Wade offered his hand to the older man. "Mr. Chatsworth. Nice to see you again."

"Surprised to see you again," the older man said, giving Wade's hand a perfunctory shake. "Thought you'd shaken the Cottonwood dust off your shoes for good."

Anne's mother elbowed her husband. "Milton, for heaven's sake. Hello, Wade. We're glad you've come back. This is our daughter, Anne. You two were just children the last time you met."

Wade took Anne's hand, holding it a shade longer than necessary. "Actually…"

Anne's eyes widened in alarm.

He gave her a teasing smile before continuing. "Actually, we ran into each other at the garden center yesterday. Sometimes I forget what a truly small town Cottonwood is. Come on out this way for the food and beer." He led her parents out to the patio, where they were immediately swallowed up by the crowd.

Anne hung back. "You didn't have to do that."

"Do what?" he asked innocently.

"Almost give me a heart attack."

"Relax, I won't give away your dirty little secret."

"You don't have to put it like that. I'm not ashamed of knowing you. I just don't want to explain what I was doing at the rodeo when I was supposed to be studying for my final exams. Oh, I have something for you.'' She reached into her voluminous purse and withdrew a tiny potted ivy. ''Somehow, in the confusion at the cash register, I ended up with one of your plants.''

''And you actually felt compelled to return it?'' Apparently she felt she'd needed an excuse to talk to him. Promising. If he was stuck in Cottonwood while his horse recovered, he could do worse than to spend that time with Anne. Plus, if she accepted him, his own family would almost have to.

''I like to tie up loose ends,'' she said. ''This concludes our business, I believe.''

''C'mon, Annie, I'm dyin' here. Won't you throw me a scrap of hope that you care something for me?'' He waggled his eyebrows at her, though the question carried more weight than he cared to admit. It really did pain him to think she cared nothing for him. In fact, he simply refused to accept that as a possibility.

''Wade, please.'' But she laughed.

Okay, now he was getting somewhere. ''You want a beer?''

''Not trying to get me drunk, I hope.''

''From what I remember, that's not necessary.''

She narrowed her eyes. ''You're not winning any points by reminding me of my unladylike behavior.''

''Oh, I think you were very ladylike. Stay here. I'll get you something to drink.'' Wade worked his way through the crowd to the kegs. He had to stand in line, but finally he was able to pour a couple of frosty cups.

He returned to where he'd left Anne, but she was gone.

''Well, damn.'' He was some kind of sucker, wandering off and leaving her alone, giving her a golden opportunity to escape him. And in this crowd, he might not find her again.

Then he saw a flash of red hair on the dance floor. It was Anne, all right, dancing the Texas two-step and laughing with her partner as she stepped on his foot. The flash of red-hot jealousy took him by surprise—especially when he realized the man who held her in his arms was none other than his brother Jeff.

"You gonna drink both those?"

Wade looked over to find Jonathan standing next to him. He silently handed his brother one of the beers, since Anne apparently had no need of it.

"They make an attractive couple," Jonathan said casually.

"Isn't Jeff here with a date?" Wade asked, irritated.

"Just Allison," Jonathan said. "They're old friends."

Wade suspected Allison wouldn't appreciate the designation of "just Allison."

Well, hell, he didn't have to stand here and watch this. He'd rather go back to the barn and talk to his horse.

"WANT SOME ICED TEA?" Jeff asked when their dance ended. "You look a little winded."

Anne didn't doubt it. That was the most exertion she'd had in weeks. "No, thanks. Actually, someone went to get me a beer a while ago..." She looked around but saw no sign of Wade. Shoot, she hadn't meant to just walk off. But when Jeff had suddenly claimed her for a dance, insisting it was his favorite song, he'd not given her a chance to say no.

The deejay put on a slow song, a Patsy Cline ballad. Jeff smoothly pulled her closer. ''How 'bout a change of pace, then?''

There was no mistaking the look in Jeff's eyes. He still had some romantic notions about her. Oh, *shoot.* She looked away, not meeting his gaze.

Automatically he put a couple of inches' distance between them. ''All right, I'll behave. But you look awfully pretty today. I hadn't realized until recently what a beautiful woman you'd grown into.''

''That's silly,'' she said. ''I'm not beautiful.''

''Have you looked in a mirror lately?''

She remembered studying herself in the mirror when she'd been dressed as Annie, thinking she *did* look pretty. But that was a costume, a character, not the real Anne. The real Anne was pleasant-looking and well-groomed, not beautiful or sexy.

''I'm sorry, I'm embarrassing you,'' Jeff said. ''I just thought, since you're here and you don't have to study or job hunt for a couple of hours, you wouldn't mind my flirting.''

''Just so you don't expect me to flirt back. I'm no good at it.'' Although Annie was. She'd been shocked at some of the things that had come out of her mouth when she'd played the part of a rodeo groupie.

''You don't have to flirt back. Just smile every once in a while, so people won't think I'm boring you.''

Anne endured the rest of the dance with him. He was very sweet and handsome, and it sure wouldn't hurt her reputation any for the people of Cottonwood to see him flirting with her. In high school she hadn't been able to *buy* a flirtation from anyone.

As soon as the song ended, however, she made her escape. What she needed was some fresh air. She got herself a canned diet drink, then let herself out the patio gate to the side yard.

Someone came right behind her. She turned, afraid it would be Jeff—or worse, Wade. But it was just Sam. He looked up at her with a snaggletoothed grin. Darn, but he was precious.

"Hi, Anne!"

"Hello, Sam. Are you having a good time?"

"Nah, I hate parties. Too many people, and there's no chocolate ice cream, only vanilla."

"No chocolate! Who catered this party, anyway? We'll put together a lynch mob and hang 'em from the nearest tree."

Sam giggled. "Hey, you want to see the frogs in their new house?"

"You finished the terrarium, huh?"

"Not all the way. It's in the barn. Come on, I'll show you."

Anne supposed it was okay for her to leave the party for a while. With so many guests, she doubted anyone would miss her.

As they made their way down the long corridor in the modern barn, a familiar whinny came from one of the stalls.

"Traveler!" Anne stopped to pet Wade's horse. She'd never been much of a rider, since she'd had a late start at this small-town-life stuff, but last May Wade had let her ride Traveler. The big, gentle horse, so responsive to the slightest pressure of knee or rein, had made her feel like an expert horsewoman. "I thought you'd be out frolicking with the mares on a pretty day like today."

She scratched his black forelock the way Wade had showed her, and he huffed in pleasure.

"He's lame," Sam said. "Grandpa Pete says he'll have to go to the glue factory."

"Oh, no!" Poor Wade. He must be devastated.

"Never mind what Grandpa Pete says," came a testy male voice from inside the stall. Wade stood, his head and shoulders appearing suddenly above the door.

Anne jumped back in surprise. "You scared the living bejeesus out of me!" Anne said with a nervous laugh. "What were you doing, hiding down there?"

"I was putting a compress on Traveler's leg," he said, opening the stall door and letting himself out, showing Anne the injured leg. "He got hurt at the rodeo in Salt Lake City. He's out of commission for a while, but a long way from being put out to pasture."

"Is that why you came back here?"

"I couldn't think of a better place for him to recuperate."

Anne's heart squeezed at the thought of poor Traveler being hurt. By the look on Wade's face, his horse's injury had hit him hard. "I never even asked you why you'd come back," she said, only now realizing how one-sided their conversation in the old hay barn had been. She'd been worried about her situation, her feelings.

It hadn't even occurred to her to wonder what Wade was doing in Cottonwood, or why he'd suddenly decided to come home when he'd sworn the family breach was impassable. "Last you told me, you and your family were barely in touch, much less on visiting terms."

Wade looked thoughtful, as if he really had to struggle to come up with an explanation for his return to Cottonwood. Finally he said, "Traveler needed a quiet place to rest, and I wanted Doc Chandler to care for him."

The answer didn't satisfy Anne, but she sensed she wouldn't get any more of an explanation from Wade, at least not today, not in front of Sam.

She turned her attention to Traveler. "Hey, big guy. Sorry to hear about that bum leg. You're going to get better, though, right?"

"I hope so," Wade answered for the horse.

She remembered the driving goal he'd told Annie about. "Wade, what about your championship?"

"I haven't lost it yet. I still have Kansas City."

"Will Traveler be healed in time?"

"I don't know."

Anne couldn't even imagine Wade's frustration. To be so close to the pinnacle of his profession and have a setback like this…

"Maybe you could ride another horse," Sam said, which was just what Anne was about to suggest.

Wade frowned. "That doesn't seem right, somehow."

"Wade, I know you're loyal to Traveler. But if he can't compete, I don't think he'd mind your riding a different horse. He'd want you to win."

That made Wade smile. "Yeah, I guess he would. But the bond between horse and rider can't be established in such a short time. I could compete with another horse, but I doubt I'd win.''

The horse huffed and stomped and swished his tail as if he agreed.

''So, you're here to see Frogville?'' Wade's abrupt change in topic didn't escape Anne. Talking about the upcoming competition made him uncomfortable.

''Sam's been telling me what a fabulous habitat you're building for Alexander and Miss Pooh.''

''Let's go have a look, then.''

This wasn't what Anne had had in mind when she'd left the party. She'd wanted to escape the Hardison brothers' testosterone, and here she was right back in the thick of things. Plus, she was having a hard time staying mad at Wade for criticizing her. His obvious concern for his horse just melted her heart.

Anyway, he was right about her, at least partly. She *was* uptight, and too serious, and she could do more with her clothes and hair. She'd simply not wanted to bother before.

WADE LET SAM LEAD THE WAY to the empty stall where he and the kids had set up the terrarium yesterday. He watched the redheaded woman and blond little boy walking down the passageway. Anne laughed again and ruffled Sam's hair. Anne Chatsworth, future lawyer, liked kids? She'd seemed real comfortable with Sam and Kristin at the garden center, which had surprised him a little, though in her Annie persona she'd claimed to love babies and animals and old people.

Maybe that part, at least, hadn't been an act.

At least she didn't seem as mad at him today. He

hoped that meant she would give him another chance. Sam's presence seemed to ease the tension between them. It was damn near impossible to exchange harsh words in front of the good-natured little boy.

Wade had found unexpected satisfaction in the bond he'd so quickly formed with his niece and nephew. He'd always enjoyed being around kids, but Sam and Kristin were the first ones he'd ever gotten close to.

Spending time with them had only cemented his latest goals. Settling down used to sound so dull and boring, the thought scared him witless. But now the idea of home and hearth, kids and a dog and a mortgage, held considerable appeal.

His time with Annie, though, was what had first gotten him thinking he could retire from rodeo sooner rather than later. Something about her had made him long for stability.

Wade covertly studied Anne and Sam as they turned into the stall where the terrarium was, and he felt an unexpected tug of an emotion he couldn't even name. The sight was just so...domestic, somehow.

Anne followed Sam into the stall. Wade was proud of their previous day's handiwork. They had set up a worktable in the stall, near a large window that let in plenty of light. They'd placed a fifty-gallon aquarium on the table, then partially filled it with sand. They'd placed a small mirror in the bottom of a green plastic bowl, then sunk the bowl into the sand and filled it with water—the frogs had their own "lake." Finally they'd transplanted some of the little plants they'd bought at the garden center into the terrarium, though the "landscaping" wasn't yet complete.

Anne peered into the terrarium, searching amongst the greenery. "I don't see—oh, there they are. Hi, frogs. Wow, you guys are living in some pretty cool digs." She looked at Sam. "What do you feed them?"

"I think they eat algae and stuff. What did you feed *your* pet frog?"

"Well, he lived in my mother's garden, so he rustled up his own grub. But I think frogs eat bugs."

"Bugs?" Sam was clearly intrigued by this idea. He immediately went to work hunting on the barn floor for some likely frog food.

Anne took a closer look at the terrarium plants. She reached inside and felt some of the leaves, a look of concern on her face.

"I'm not sure I did a good job planting them," Wade said. "I'm no gardener, and my hands are too big and clumsy to work in that small space."

Anne gave him a measured look. "I don't know about clumsy..." And for just a moment she was Annie, flirting with him. Abruptly she put a lid on *that* line of discussion.

She cleared her throat. "I think a little water's all they need." She sprinkled some water from a watering can into the terrarium. "Heads up, frogs. It's monsoon season."

"Hey, I found an ant," Sam said. He came over to the terrarium with a small black ant crawling on his hand and brushed it off. It landed on a large, flat rock.

Alexander and Miss Pooh were intrigued and excited by the new food source. It took them only a few moments to figure out what to do. Miss Pooh was faster, and with a tongue longer than her whole body, she zapped the ant and swallowed it in one gulp.

Judging from the giggles, it was the funniest thing Sam had ever seen. Wade laughed right along with him, and Anne joined in until tears formed in her eyes.

"Hey, how 'bout that?" Wade said when he could talk. "We got the Nature Channel right here in our own barn."

"I gotta tell Dad and Kristin!" Sam announced, darting out of the stall.

Now, this was more like it. Alone at last with Anne.

She didn't look appreciative of their sudden privacy. In fact, she got that scared-rabbit glint in her eyes.

"Well, um, that *was* pretty funny." She folded her arms, refusing to look at him.

"Looks like we'll have to catch some ants. We might have starved the poor frogs if you hadn't come along."

Only, he was the one who was starving—starving for Anne's touch.

Chapter Five

"I'd better get back to the party," Anne said, turning resolutely toward the stall door, intending to avoid temptation.

Wade caught her by the arm, playfully spinning her around. "What's your hurry?"

"No hurry. I just don't want to be rude."

"The crowd is so huge at the house, no one will miss you. Except maybe...Jeff?"

"Why would Jeff miss me?" she asked too quickly, too brightly.

"The way you two were dancing, I was surprised you didn't both leave the party. Together."

"Oh, Wade, don't be ridiculous. Jeff and I are friends. He's like my big brother."

"Brothers don't slow dance with their sisters."

Wade was jealous! The thought sent a tingly thrill up her spine, which she was immediately ashamed of. "I'm not going to stand here and justify my friendship with your brother."

"You don't have to. You and I don't have any kind of understanding between us. You made that real clear."

He was challenging her to deny there was anything between them. She opened her mouth to do just that, but no words at all, not even the wrong ones, would form while he was so close, looking so darn masculine in those faded jeans and flannel shirt. His clothes looked butter-soft from too many washings, and all she could think about was touching him.

Which would be very easy to do, since he'd closed in on her, backing her up against the wall. He placed one hand against the wall on either side of her, so he was right in her face but not touching.

"Why do you wear those clothes?" he asked.

"What's wrong with my clothes? You keep harping on that. I shop at good stores."

"That may be, but your clothes are baggy. I think you dress like you do to keep men away."

"Then it's not working very well, is it?" Her voice was thready, pleading. She did not want to face this…this *need* she had—so unseemly, so *not* her.

"And I think you wear your hair all slicked back for the same reason." He reached behind her and grabbed the end of her braid. With one quick yank he removed the elastic band. Immediately the braid started to unravel.

"Wade!" She frantically tried to rebraid the pigtail, but she realized it was a lost cause. Escaping this barn was a lost cause. He had her and he knew it.

"Tell me you don't want to get back what we had."

She couldn't.

"Didn't think so." With that Wade claimed the kiss he'd been inching toward, and Anne was helpless to prevent it. Her heart thumped wildly as their lips met and his warmth surrounded her like molasses. She knew she should object, but she couldn't seem to find a logical reason to.

She abandoned her attempt to braid her hair and gave herself to the kiss, which was gentle and insistent, warm and welcoming, yet demanding. Wade slid his tongue into her mouth and pressed his body against hers in a seductive rhythm that left no doubt where he wanted to go with this kiss.

A kiss like that could make a woman remember. Anne remembered a cowboy's long, lean body pressed up against hers, no clothes between them...remembered the giddy abandon that had brought them to that point...remembered the bold caresses, the tender words.

Such a kiss could also make her forget everything that had happened over the past few months. She could easily forget everything except being here with Wade.

Somehow she managed to break the kiss. "Wade, we have to stop this."

"Why?" He gave her ear a playful nip, sending shivers all the way into her fingernails.

She relied on the quickest, easiest excuse. "Because we aren't in a private place. Sam could be back anytime, with Kristin, and this isn't the sort of display I want to foist on children."

He tensed, immediately halting his sensual assault on her ear. "Darn it, I hate it when you're right."

She thought for a moment she'd dodged the bullet. He was going to let her go. But in the next moment he swung her up into his arms and carried her out of the stall.

"Wh-what—" she sputtered. "Wade, stop it. Put me down."

"In a minute." He kissed her to silence her protestations, and she closed her eyes and took what he offered. A few seconds' darkness enveloped them, along with the scent of leather and saddle soap, and she realized Wade had carried her into a tack room.

He didn't turn on the light, apparently knowing exactly where he was going. Next thing she knew she was lying on what felt like a pile of blankets and Wade was closing and locking the door.

She had no protests left. She wanted this as badly as he did. He joined her on the blankets.

"Hmm, now where were we?" He kissed her again, more fervently, with the supreme confidence of a male who'd made a conquest. Not that she'd been much of a challenge, Anne thought dazedly as Wade's hand slid under her sweater. His hand stopped short of her breast, caressing her ribs and back.

She didn't want him to take his time. She wanted him fast and furious, now, before her good sense returned, before someone interrupted them. The smell of his skin, where she'd buried her face in that special place just under his jaw, made her warm with longing. She tasted his neck, wanting more, wanting all of him at once.

He groaned and at last placed a hand over one of her breasts. The contact was exquisite, sending starbursts of pleasure all over her body like shooting stars.

"Too many clothes," he murmured, and set about remedying that situation. He pulled her sweater over her head, getting her elbow caught in the sleeve in his hurry. They both laughed as she tried to untrap herself.

"Shh," she said through her giggles. "Someone could hear."

"Let 'em," Wade said, but he did quiet down. The rest of their clothes flew off in record time. It was like the first time they'd made love, she remembered, frantic and fevered, except this time she knew how good it would be.

As more and more of her skin was bared to his touch, she could feel goose bumps break out all over her body—not from the cold, though it was pretty cold in that tack room.

Wade kissed her mouth, her neck, her breasts, her stomach, all the while stroking her body with feathery fingers, driving her slowly out of her mind.

"Now," she pleaded.

"I know," he said. "Me, too. I've got to get—" He stopped touching her long enough to feel around the floor for his jeans.

Should she tell him? Yes, definitely. "We don't need a condom," she blurted out. "I'm on the pill." Jeff had suggested she take precautions against future unplanned pregnancies. In no mood to argue, she'd blithely done whatever he told her, even though at that time she didn't imagine she would want to have sex ever, ever again.

Thank you, Jeff.

Wade greeted her announcement with silence at first. Then, "Are you, now?"

"Yes, oh, please, I want you now, Wade." Was that actually her voice, pleading for sex? The man made her insane.

"You know what to say," he teased as he reclaimed his spot on the blankets beside her, pulling her close.

"You're not going to make me—"

"I want to hear it."

She sighed, cursing that silly part of her that was Annie. "I want my big boy," she said, through an embarrassed giggle.

He rolled on top of her and she widened her legs to make room. Oh, yes, yes, this felt so right. She'd forgotten how good it felt to have the essence of this man all over her, inside her, a part of her.

"You say it, too," she whispered as they rocked together.

"I've got my sweet girl," he whispered back, and Anne had never heard more wonderful words in her life. They climaxed together, as they'd done from the very first time, so completely in tune with each other's bodies it was almost as if they really were one.

Afterward they lay together in silence. Anne reveled in the sound of Wade's breathing. Funny, how one person's breath could sound unique. She would try to remember that sound and conjure it up when she was alone at night.

"I really should get back to the party," she said again.

This time he didn't argue. He sat up when she did, helped her find her clothes in the dark. They dressed quietly, absorbing the wonder of their coupling.

"Is there a bathroom in the barn?" Anne asked. She needed to freshen up a bit before rejoining the party. "I've got to fix my hair."

"You sure worry a lot about what people think."

"I guess I do." All she needed was for her parents to hear she'd been rolling around in the hay with a rodeo cowboy. That would just ice the cake of her father's loss of confidence in her judgment.

Wade showed her to the bathroom. When she was done, she opened the door and peeked out to see that the coast was clear before emerging.

Wade laughed at her. "You look like a guilty teenager."

"I feel like one. Next time let's not do this in the middle of a party." Belatedly she realized what she'd said. *Next time.*

Wade caught it, too. "Will there be a next time?"

She hesitated. Her smart, practical side wanted to say no. They'd given in to an unwise impulse here. But how could she revert to that straitlaced attitude when her body was still thrumming with pleasure?

She needed to plant her feet firmly back on the ground. She hadn't made love with Wade in order to reestablish their short-lived relationship. Romantic flings constituted instant pleasure. Having once succumbed, and paid the price, she now believed more strongly than ever in delaying gratification. School, career, then fun and games and marriage and children.

Children. That brought her back to square one.

"C'mon, Annie," Wade said, his voice soft, cajoling as he touched her face, running one finger along her jaw. "I want to be with you. I'm not asking you for a lifetime. I just want to build a few memories. You're not immune to me—you just proved it."

She took a step back from him. "Physical desire isn't always under our control. And by itself, it's not a very good basis for making decisions."

"Lawyer Anne has spoken?"

"Yes, and her decision is final." She sounded about as firm as overcooked spaghetti.

Wade recognized her wishy-washiness for what it was. "Don't I get an appeal?" he cajoled.

Gosh darn it! Why did he have to be so irresistible?

"Live a little, Annie. In a few weeks you'll be off to lawyer land. I don't know that much about it, but I hear they work new lawyers like dogs. You won't have time for a social life."

"I don't have time for one now," she said.

"Ah, but you do. Maybe not a lot, but you can't tell me you don't have an hour here, an hour there. And poor ol' Wade, just hanging around with nothing to do, could be at your beck and call. Cowboy Valium at your service."

She took a deep breath. "Don't get me wrong, Wade. I love being with you, truly I do. I think a lot of you. But in case you hadn't noticed, I have no self-control when you're around."

"So? What's the worst that can happen? You lose control. We've already seen you can survive that."

Oh, no, there were far worse things than losing control. This was a good time to remind herself of that. "I need self-control. It's who I am. Having a no-commitment fling just isn't me. I'm not comfortable with it. Ultimately it would make me feel bad about myself. I just can't deal with having an affair. And I really, really need to get back to the party."

"I know, I know," he said wearily, "Your parents will worry about you."

"They will. I'm not kidding. They're wonderful people, but I'd forgotten how suffocating it can be, living under their roof."

WADE LET ANNE WALK back to the house by herself. She might think she'd gotten in the last word, but she was wrong. He wasn't giving up on her. He would just have to figure out some other way to convince her they belonged together.

Whoa. *Belonged together?* Wasn't he getting a little carried away here? Last he'd checked, all he wanted—all that was possible—was a fling. Sure, he and Anne were good together, but what exactly did he want from the woman?

Apparently more than a few nights' pleasure. He'd had that once, and it wasn't nearly enough. But how could it be more, when they would both be taking off for parts unknown in a matter of weeks?

He stood at the barn door, staring after her as she walked up to the house.

"You must have it bad."

Jonathan's voice behind him startled Wade. He whirled around to face his brother, the fight-or-flight syndrome tensing his hands into fists, until he realized who it was. He relaxed, marveling at his overreaction.

"Sorry," he said. "Guess I was in another world. What are you doing down here?" Wade realized Jonathan must have been in the office with the door closed when he and Anne had come out of the tack room. Had he heard them? Did he know?

"I needed to make a phone call," Jonathan said, "and it was too noisy at the house. So who were you out here seducing?"

Wade chafed at the insult, though he was relieved

Jonathan hadn't pegged Anne. She seemed very intent on protecting her privacy, and he would honor her wishes. "It was nobody you need to know about. And why do you assume I was seducing? Maybe I was just showing her Sam and Kristin's pet frogs."

Jonathan reached up and pulled a piece of hay out of Wade's hair. He let it go on the breeze without comment.

So much for denial.

"Now, I know you're gonna get all testy," Jonathan said, "me asking you this, but if you're all soft on this mystery woman, what exactly are you offering her—besides fun and games, that is?"

Wade refused to let his brother's needling get to him. Not this time. He knew what Jonathan was getting at, and he wasn't taking the bait.

"You don't know as much about me as you think," Wade said. Jonathan especially didn't know about the two-hundred-plus grand Wade had socked away at a brokerage firm. Prize money plus the occasional paycheck, invested well, had netted him a decent-size nest egg. Some women might find that mighty attractive, although he doubted Anne was one of them. "You'd be surprised what I could offer a woman."

"Yeah, lots of women like living in a horse trailer."

"That's kind of cold, Jon."

Jonathan looked down at the concrete floor and kicked a pebble. "I didn't bring it up to be nasty. Couples have to have something in common besides raging hormones. I learned that lesson the hard way."

Wade supposed that was true enough. Rita, Jonathan's ex-wife, had been a city girl through and through. Jon's way of life just hadn't been her cup of tea. It had been their parents' marriage, all over again, except Rita hadn't stayed.

"Anyway, you know what I was leading up to," Jonathan said.

"You want me to settle down here and work the ranch."

"I'd pay you good money."

This was an old argument. Ranch work was what had driven him away from Cottonwood and the Hardison clan in the first place. That and his family's refusal to consider his wants, his opinions or his dreams. Pete and Jonathan had adamantly refused to let him use ranch livestock for rodeo, proclaiming it a waste of time and a risk to the animals.

So he'd saved up his money and bought Traveler, an untried colt with nebulous bloodlines.

He'd be damned if he would ever herd cattle and set fence posts and castrate calves.

Still, he didn't respond to Jonathan's suggestion in anger, not this time. There was a certain comfort in knowing that as an adult he could simply say no.

"Not interested. Besides, it wouldn't help with this lady. She's not sticking around Cottonwood for long."

Wade walked away before his brother could interrogate him further. He was anxious to see what his little Annie was up to now.

Back at the party, the dance floor had expanded. It seemed everyone had gotten into the act. Even Pete was dancing with Sally, whirling the tall, wiry woman around as if she was a feather.

Wade considered asking Anne to dance. No one

would even blink, since everybody was dancing with everybody, but he thought better of it. Holding her in his arms, he wouldn't be able to behave, and he knew how sensitive she was about gossip and speculation.

Still, it almost killed him when she danced with Jonathan, then Jeff again, then one of the ranch hands. She was the unexpected belle of the ball, and he couldn't touch her. He danced with Allison, though all she did was watch Jeff dancing with Molly, the nurse from his clinic. But after that he gave up and found a beer to suck on.

Then it struck him. Much as he hated to admit it, Jonathan was right. He might have a lot to offer a woman, but had he mentioned any of it to Anne? No. Had he mentioned anything but fun and games? No. No wonder she'd said forget it.

If he wanted Anne Chatsworth, he was going to have to lay it on the line.

ANNE GOT HERSELF a cold drink and sat down with Allison, who looked a little glum, though she managed to smile a greeting.

"You're looking great," Allison said. "I'm glad to see you bouncing back. My friend had a miscarriage, and she was a mess for six months."

Anne's drink went down the wrong way. She coughed and sputtered a moment with Allison looking on, concerned.

"I'm okay," Anne said when she could breathe.

"Did I say something wrong?"

"No, no, it's just—how did you—"

"When I fixed that cavity for you last summer—

you told me you were pregnant. You were worried about the anesthetic, remember?"

"Of course, that's right." Silently Anne wondered how many other people knew about her pregnancy.

"I'm sorry," Allison said, genuinely distressed. "I'm always sticking my foot in my mouth. I guess bringing up a woman's miscarriage isn't polite party conversation."

Anne smiled. "It's okay, really. I just haven't talked about it much. You know, it's kind of a secret."

"Oh." Allison looked a little worried.

"What?"

"Well, it's not much of a secret, really. I'm afraid Cottonwood has a grapevine that could choke the whole state of Texas. Everybody knows."

Everybody? "But how?" Anne asked, feeling sick to her stomach. "I only told a few people."

"It only takes one to start the gossip mill. And it wasn't me, by the way. But try not to worry too much. It's old news. Now everyone's talking about Wade Hardison coming back to town after all these years. He sure grew up handsome. But then, all the Hardison boys turned out pretty easy on the eyes."

Anne was hardly listening. All she could think about was what if Wade got wind of her pregnancy? It wouldn't take a rocket scientist to put two and two together.

She could not imagine a worse way to discover you'd almost become a father than to hear it on a street corner as idle gossip.

She would have to tell Wade about how he wouldn't be a father.

She supposed she'd been moving toward that conclusion all along. Telling him would be one of the hardest things she'd ever done. The news would tear out his heart—she knew it would. He would have every right to be angry with her for withholding the news.

And he had a right to know.

But not today, not so soon after making love. She wanted to savor that memory, unmarred by anger, for at least a little while. Tomorrow would be soon enough.

WADE WAS AT THE BARN the next day, feeding Traveler, when Jonathan called to him from the office. "You got a phone call."

Now, who would be calling him? He headed for the office, where Jonathan held the cordless phone out to him with a knowing smirk.

"It's *her,*" Jonathan whispered.

"Who?"

"The mystery woman. She wouldn't leave her name."

Wade grabbed the phone. "Hello?"

"Wade, it's me."

"Ah." Anne. His breathing quickened at the mere sound of her voice. He stepped out of the office, ignoring Jonathan's curious look. "Change your mind about us?"

"We need to meet."

His hopes soared. "You say where and when."

"Antonio's, out on Highway 76. Noon?"

She couldn't have chosen a more out-of-the-way spot for their rendezvous. She really, really didn't want anyone to see them together. Wade didn't know whether to be insulted or intrigued, but he'd do whatever it took to see her.

"Noon it is."

"Okay, see you then." She hung up before he could ask her what this was about, but he supposed he'd find out soon enough. Noon was only a couple of hours away. He wasn't wild about the idea of meeting at a restaurant. In a public place, with a wide expanse of table between them, Anne Chatsworth, future lawyer, could reason her way into or out of any argument.

He needed her in his arms. Kissing her, holding her, loving her—that was how he made his best arguments. But he'd take what he could get.

Actually, maybe a lunch date wasn't such a bad idea. They could talk, like a real couple. He wanted sex, sure, but he also wanted to learn everything about her—*her,* Anne Chatsworth, as well as the Annie part of herself she kept hidden. Maybe the two together would be an even better package than wild Annie.

And he wanted her to know him—all of him, even the soft, vulnerable parts of his personality that embarrassed him. It was hard to trust her after she'd walked out on him once, but he knew if he didn't open himself to her, she would never understand how right they were together.

He sauntered back into the office and put the phone on its cradle. Jonathan looked up from his paperwork. "You aren't going to tell me who it is?"

"Nope. The lady requests discretion."

Jonathan just shook his head. More evidence that his brother didn't live up to Hardison family expectations.

Chapter Six

Shortly before noon, Anne slipped into her bedroom to get ready for her meeting with Wade. If her luck held out, she wouldn't have to explain where she was going. Her father was out on the lake with his newest speedboat, and her mother was at a garden club meeting.

She'd decided, though, that she wouldn't lie—she would simply insist on maintaining her privacy. Wade had hit his mark when he'd said she was acting like a teenager. Granted, she didn't want to upset her parents or worry them, but she was twenty-five years old, which meant she wasn't responsible to her parents anymore.

She would follow her father's advice when it came to her law career. But her personal life was her business, and hers alone.

Anne assessed her appearance in the mirror. Navy slacks, button-down shirt, gray cardigan sweater. Hair held back in a barrette.

Frumpy, no doubt about it. Maybe Wade was right. Maybe she did deliberately downplay her sexuality.

Because what if she tried to be sexy and failed? Was that what she'd been afraid of?

Impulsively she pulled the barrette out of her hair and fluffed out the mass of red curls. She added more makeup and a pair of dangly silver earrings, a birthday gift from one of her law school buddies.

The image that looked back at her from the mirror wasn't a stranger, exactly—more like a friend she hadn't seen in a while. About five months, to be specific. The clothes were still conservative, but the woman in the mirror—at least from the neck up—could in no way be called a frump.

Deborah was just pulling into the garage as Anne headed for her car. Anne steeled herself, remembering her earlier determination that she owned her own personal life.

"Oh, Anne, good, I'm glad I caught you," Deborah said as she climbed out of the Cadillac. "I was just talking to—" She stopped midsentence to stare at her daughter. "Good heavens, Anne, what have you done to yourself?"

Anne smiled, embarrassed at being caught with her vanity, and gave her head a shake, causing the earrings to tinkle like mini wind chimes. "I was in a funky mood."

Deborah focused on Anne's face. "I'm not sure that lipstick shade is best for your coloring."

Anne shrugged. "I'm not, either, but the world won't come to an end if I wear the wrong lipstick." She scooted past Deborah and headed for her own car. "I need to run, I'm already late."

"Where are you off to?" Deborah asked, sounding a little anxious.

"Lunch with a friend. Back in a couple of hours." *Please, no more questions.*

"Would this be a male friend?"

Anne stopped, turned and, remembering her decision to be honest, said very deliberately, "Yes. And I'm late."

"Someone you met at the party?"

Had her mother realized she and Wade were gone at the same time yesterday? But the question seemed innocent enough.

"We'll talk later," Anne said, knowing she was only delaying the inevitable cross-examination. Deborah was at least as good as her husband when it came to rooting out information from unwilling sources, although her father would probably join in if Deborah told him his darling daughter was off carousing with the opposite sex. But between now and later, Anne would figure out how to explain her behavior.

When she pulled her Mustang into the pizza parlor's parking lot, she found Wade was already there, sitting on the hood of his beat-up pickup truck—which was the only other vehicle in the lot.

She soon figured out why. The restaurant was closed, boarded up, and had a For Sale sign on the roof.

"Annie?" he asked uncertainly.

"It's still Anne," she replied firmly. "I was just tired of you thinking I'm a sexless frump."

"You look great. The clothes could use some work—"

"Hey!"

"But the hair is perfect." He nodded toward the restaurant. "We'll have to go with plan B."

"What's plan B?" She probably shouldn't have asked. She should have just made an alternate suggestion right away.

"It's too nice a day to stay inside," Wade said, hopping down from the truck and giving her a peck on the cheek. "Why don't we grab a bucket of chicken and have a picnic?"

Her cheek burned where his lips had touched. Maybe she shouldn't have done her hair this way. She was feeling more and more like Annie, and Annie always had naughty things on her mind. Today was about talking, not…well, not other things.

"A picnic where?" Not in Town Square Park, she hoped. Though it was a beautiful spot, everybody and their mother would see them.

"I know just the place. Hop in." He opened the truck's passenger door.

This wasn't how she'd planned for their lunch to go. But she couldn't come up with a logical objection, other than admit she was afraid to be alone with him, afraid she couldn't trust herself. If she found herself in Wade's arms, all of her good intentions about honesty and full disclosure would fly right out the window.

She wondered just how private his intended picnic spot would be.

A few minutes later she had her answer. With the fragrant bucket of spicy chicken between them, Wade drove his truck past the Hardison Ranch for about half a mile, then turned down a pitted dirt road. They passed a farm with a big, rambling house and sign that said, Horses Boarded. Anne studied the two-story house with its inviting front porch. It was run-down but still charming. Another farmer trying to hold on to his land, renting out pasture to make ends meet. It was a common story around here.

"That's where Sally Enderlin lives," Wade said, noticing Anne's attention. "After my mom died, Sally practically raised me. She and Pete are sweet on each other, have been for years. But they're both too proud to admit it."

Sweet on each other. Anne liked that phrase. It hearkened back to a simpler time. She and Wade weren't sweet on each other. They were hot on each other.

Anne recalled seeing Sally at the party—seventyish but still youthful, always laughing about something, her mop of white hair dyed blond. "I know Sally. She was involved in the 4-H Club when I was a member."

"You were 4-H?"

She shrugged. "Another of my doomed attempts to fit in with some crowd or another. It's hard to pretend you're a farm kid when you live on the lake, though."

"I didn't fit into 4-H, either. Every year Jonathan gave me a calf to raise. But I hated all that grooming, all those prissy cows standing around looking pretty for the judges. All I cared about was riding horses and riding 'em fast."

Now why didn't that surprise her?

Wade turned onto an even smaller road, where they bounced over huge potholes even when he slowed the truck to a crawl. Obviously, the road was seldom used.

"Is this private property?" she wondered aloud.

"Yeah. It's part of the ranch, but it's too rough for grazing. Pete keeps threatening to sell it off, but every time he thinks about developers coming in here and tearing out all the trees to build tract homes, he changes his mind."

"It's really beautiful." And secluded. The pine trees were thick and tall, shielding them from any possible observation. Wade had probably chosen this spot for that very reason. The thought sent a pleasurable chill wiggling up her spine and radiating through her shoulders and stomach and hips—especially her hips.

No, no, no. She couldn't touch him, couldn't kiss him, *could not* make love with him. Yesterday the whole sex thing had taken her by surprise. She hadn't had a chance to think about it. But now that she'd decided to tell Wade about the baby, sex would have to wait.

Her earlier lack of responsibility had caused her to conceive a child that never should have been conceived. That was one experience she couldn't live through again.

After she told him about the baby, about how she'd intended to have it without his knowing, he probably would never want to touch her again. The thought made her chest ache. No matter what, she didn't want Wade to hate her.

Wade pulled the truck off the road and cut the engine. "This is the place."

They got out of the truck and climbed up a small rise, then stood on low limestone bluffs overlooking a gurgling creek that widened and pooled below them. Nature had provided a large, flat rock just begging for a picnic blanket. Spots of warm sunlight peeked through the canopy of leaves.

"Misspent a good portion of my youth here," Wade said. "Check out the tire swing."

An old tire was suspended on a long, thick rope above the pool. "This must have been paradise for kids during summer vacation."

"It's always been my favorite place. I used to sneak out here to avoid ranch work," he admitted. "Pete declared it off-limits, and more than once he cut down the tire swing, but I always put a new one up. Guess he finally gave up."

Anne could easily remember Wade as he'd looked when she'd first met him as a teenager—lanky but already broad-shouldered, with dark, shaggy hair and those intense eyes—defying authority by escaping to this cool oasis on a scorching summer day.

He looked out at the creek, remembering something that put a wistful, half smile on his face. With an uncomfortable pang, she realized she could not tell Wade about their baby in this place, his special place. If she did, she would ruin it with painful memories.

The explanation would have to wait.

"Did you bring girls here?" she asked.

He gave her a look. "What do you think?"

She supposed the answer was yes. This was also an ideal place for seduction, if the weather cooperated. Like it did today. She decided not to pursue that line of thought.

They spread out a couple of old horse blankets onto the flat rock—why horse blankets? she thought in despair. Then he unpacked the feast, which made Anne's mouth water just from looking. Crisp fried chicken, creamy potato salad, crunchy dill pickle spears and moist, crumbly brownies.

They ate everything, washing it down with sweetened iced tea. And they talked about all kinds of things. The easy conversation made her think of their weekend in Dallas, when they'd talked so much they almost went hoarse. Except then she'd been posing as Annie, and she'd revealed very little of her true life. Freed from that constraint, she found herself babbling about things she'd never told anyone—how left out she'd felt in high school, how she'd finally made close friends in college, only to lose them when she'd graduated. And how scared she'd been those first few weeks at SMU law school.

Anne made a token effort to help Wade clean up their lunch leavings, but he told her to relax. This was his treat for her.

Oddly enough, she *was* able to relax. As long as she didn't think about the secret she was keeping from him, that is.

When everything was packed away, Wade sat down next to her. He said nothing, just stared out over the creek, his expression thoughtful. If Anne hadn't known better, she'd have thought Wade pondered weightier issues than she did.

"It seemed like you had something important on your mind when you called me this morning," he finally said. "Somehow, I don't think it was so you could tell me about being the only senior in high school with braces."

Anne felt her face heat. How could she explain her behavior? Her phone call earlier had held a decidedly urgent note to it. She'd been determined to get the information out in the open. Now she was just as determined to keep quiet about it. There was a time and a place for everything, and this wasn't it.

"C'mon, Annie. Spit it out."

"I...um...well, it's not that important."

He smiled at her. "Can I guess?"

"No!" This wasn't a game.

"I will, anyway. I'm guessing that you changed your mind. About us." He flashed a heart-melting smile at her. "You've thought about how good we are together, and you're not quite ready to turn your back on that. Am I right?"

"Yes!" She seized on the explanation he came up with. "That's exactly it. I want to have a...meaningless fling with you."

"Oh, Annie, you wound me. Meaningless? That's not what I want, at all. Yeah, I want to make love to you. Lots and lots. But I want more than that."

Anne suddenly couldn't get enough air. What was going on here? Where was that sexy cowboy with only the next conquest on his mind?

"There's something special between us," he went on. "Whether you call yourself Anne or Annie, whether you're dressed sexy or frumpy, whether you're a cowgirl or lawyer, that doesn't change."

"We do have a rare chemistry," she agreed. A bead of perspiration trickled between her breasts even though the temperature was moderate.

"It's not just a physical reaction, although we certainly have that. It's something bigger, something we shouldn't just chuck out the window because our lives don't knit together very well right now."

A pretty speech was the last thing she'd expected

from Wade Hardison...and the last thing she could cope with right now. She'd been prepared for seduction. But she could do nothing to stop this assault on her emotions. Apparently she'd misjudged him... again.

"Wade, please—"

"I know what you're going to say. We're from two different worlds. You're educated and sophisticated and wealthy, and I'm just a hayseed—"

"I would never say anything like that!"

"You might not say it, but you can't help but think it. I've thought about the differences between us, too. But we have a lot in common. You can't deny that."

No, she couldn't. Their long-winded chat over lunch had proved that. She found him intelligent, funny, well-read—he killed time by reading when he was on the road, everything from bestsellers to the classics. They liked the same foods, the same movies. She liked the music he listened to.

Mostly she liked the way he touched her.

"We'll be going our separate ways pretty soon," he continued. "But does that have to mean we say goodbye forever?"

"I don't see how it could mean anything else."

"When people want to be together, they find ways."

"Long-distance relationships rarely work out," she reminded him.

"Rarely, but sometimes they do. We won't know till we try."

Wade's sincere request that they give their relationship a chance affected her as no skilled seduction could have. How many guys would be willing to put themselves out on a limb like Wade just had? To risk all kinds of rejection and humiliation from a woman he really didn't know that well?

The way he looked at her with those big brown eyes, patiently waiting for her to answer, just about did her in. She was utterly helpless to resist. At this particular moment he could have her—anything he wanted from her.

"Just promise me you'll think about it."

She didn't want to think, because that was too painful. She just wanted to feel. Instead of answering, she leaned in and kissed him.

He didn't object. In fact, when he recovered from his surprise and kissed her back, it seemed as natural as breathing. It was always like that with them. When he was close like this, his body became almost an extension of her own, it felt so right.

He kissed her more gently than he had in the barn, with a lazy attitude, as if they had all the time in the world. Hazily she recalled that she didn't have all day—she had letters to write, constitutional law to memorize.

But somehow none of that seemed as pressing as it should have. She was here, with Wade, in the most lovely spot on earth, and nothing else mattered.

Wade angled his body closer to hers and tangled his hand in her hair, holding her steady for a more focused sensual assault. Her breasts ached where they rubbed against his chest. She tangled her legs up with his in an effort to bring their bodies closer still.

He stopped kissing her, prompting her to open her eyes. She found him staring into her face, his expression serious, his brown eyes dark and intense.

WADE SAW SOMETHING in Anne's gaze that troubled him. It was that sadness he'd noticed at Autumn Daze.

There was something dark in her soul, something she didn't want to share with him.

He'd taken a huge chance by bringing Anne here, by declaring he wanted them to be together, a couple, not just for a few days or a couple of weeks.

At least she hadn't laughed at the idea. But she hadn't jumped at his offer, either. He got the idea that she was intrigued by it, but something held her back. And it wasn't just their overt differences.

She closed her eyes again and parted her lips slightly. Unable to resist, he took the kiss she offered. And he immediately got the idea that she wanted more than a kiss. Was this the consolation prize, then? Her way of telling him this was all they could have—the here and now?

She kissed his ear, then ran her tongue along the edge, and he had a hard time holding on to any coherent thought. For someone who dressed like a prep school headmistress, she had some awesome powers of seduction. And maybe more sex was the best thing for them, after all. He'd read somewhere that women couldn't have sex without their emotions getting all tied up in it. He was all for tying up Anne's emotions, since his were already in big, fat knots.

She threw her arms around him, pushing him back down to the blanket and kissing him with the abandon he remembered from months ago.

She unbuttoned his shirt, kissing each new spot she uncovered on his chest. She unbuckled his belt and unfastened his Wranglers with nimble fingers, having suddenly lost any vestiges of shyness.

He gasped with pleasure when she demonstrated exactly how seductive she could be. She got him so worked up in record time, he was afraid this whole delightful interlude would be over too soon if he didn't do something. So he grabbed her around the middle and tickled her.

"Oh! You're likely to get hurt tickling me when you're in such a vulnerable position." She collapsed onto her back, giggling like Kristin did when he tickled her. But she sure didn't feel like a little girl.

He stopped tickling and covered her breasts with his palms. She gasped, and the amusement left her eyes, replaced by sultry desire. He flicked open the row of tiny buttons on her gray sweater, then her blouse, revealing a plunge-front, hot-pink bra.

Just the sight of her milky breasts spilling out of the undergarment was enough to make him almost lose control. That was one thing he remembered about Annie—her sensible underthings. Though she'd been hot as a firecracker on the outside, her bra and panties had been plain white cotton, which had surprised him.

"Is this what you bought at Hollywood Lingerie?" he asked, running his finger along the tops of her breasts, then casually unhooking the front clasp.

"Yes. And matching panties."

"Bikini?"

"Thong."

He could have melted into a puddle right then and there. Anne in a hot-pink thong. "I have to see." He immediately went to work on her shoes and socks, then her pants, which refused to budge past her hips.

"Did you have these things sewn on to you or

what?'' he groused good-naturedly as he gave the pants another tug.

''Are you insinuating I'm fat?''

''You're perfect,'' he said. Although now that he thought about it, she did seem a little more rounded than she had back in May. More womanly. Her mother was probably feeding her better at home than Anne had fed herself at school.

Finally he got the pants off, and he paused to admire the picture of Anne in her hot-pink Hollywood ensemble. The panties were so brief they barely covered her thatch of dark-red curls.

''Let me see the back,'' he said, his voice almost a growl.

''No.'' She abruptly went all shy on him, blushing prettily all over her whole body.

''C'mon. You wore them for me, didn't you?''

''I wore them for me. I wanted to feel feminine and sexy.''

''Liar.'' With one fluid movement he stood, pulling her up with him. Once she was on her feet, it was easy to twirl her around so he could see her backside, left almost completely bare by her abbreviated underwear.

''Now that is a beautiful sight.''

''Come on, Wade, you're making me feel icky.''

Icky. That was a word Annie would use. He liked it. ''Icky, how?''

''Like an exhibitionist. I mean, out here in broad daylight. What if someone came along?''

''No one ever comes out here. Your exhibit—'' and he fondled her bare hip to make a point ''—is for me, and me only.''

He kissed her again, not teasing this time. She kissed him back without reservation, and he marveled at the degree of trust she showed him.

Somehow they ended up lying on the blanket again. Anne made quick work of his clothes and her underthings until they were both lying naked on the old horse blanket in a patch of sunlight. While kissing her breasts, he teased her legs open with one hand, then made a leisurely exploration, letting her gasps and whimpers guide him.

She always felt right to him, as if she belonged to him, as if they were meant to lie like this, their bodies designed solely for mutual pleasure. The rightness of it took his breath away. Or that might have been Anne's fingers doing their own exploration.

"Lie back and relax," he coaxed her.

"But—"

"There'll be time enough for me later."

Kissing away her objections, he devoted himself to bringing her pleasure, letting his fingers dance over her skin and dip into her most private places. He brought her to a climax almost immediately, thoroughly enjoying her body's response to his ministrations. She stifled her cries of ecstasy, just as she'd done in the barn, even though there was no one around for miles. But there was no mistaking what was happening to her body. She wiggled and writhed until just watching her quivering flesh was almost too much stimulation for Wade's hungry body.

"I was just getting warmed up," he admonished her as he gathered her into his arms. He loved her this way, soft and utterly vulnerable, her trust in him complete. He brushed a strand of damp hair off her forehead, then kissed her there, finding her skin slightly salty.

"If that's just a warm-up, I can't wait for the finale."

"Is that an invitation?"

"For some future time. If you touched me again now, I'd...I'd vaporize."

"I'll hold you to that—the future date, not the vaporizing part."

She snuggled up against him, inadvertently rubbing that part of him that was already primed for action. Or maybe not so inadvertently, he realized as she did it again, then caressed him with her hand.

"My turn," she whispered, and he was at her mercy. Her sensual assault drove him straight out of his mind, straight to a place he could almost call heaven.

Anne had never applied herself like this before. During their crazy weekend, they'd always been eager to join in mutual pleasure. It was a turn-on, her showering all her attention on him while he relaxed and did nothing.

It was over too soon, but he clung to the fact that she'd left the door open. "At some future time," she'd said. Was tomorrow future enough? How about tonight?

"WHY DON'T YOU COME riding with me next week?" Wade asked casually.

Anne's first instinct was to jump at the invitation. Anything to be with this man, who literally made her forget who she was. Still, she couldn't help her natural caution creeping in. "I'm not a very good rider."

"We'll find a mount you can handle. You did fine with Traveler."

"But he's so gentle."

"Jonathan has lots of gentle horses."

It wasn't just the riding that made her apprehensive. How could she possibly go riding on the Hardison ranch without Wade's family seeing her?

"I need to study," she tried again.

"Bring your books over. I'll help you study."

She laughed, then stopped when he looked offended. "You're serious?"

"You think I'm such an intellectual lightweight I couldn't be of any help?"

"I just think you'd be bored to tears."

"I won't be. Next objection?"

She couldn't bring herself to tell him her real concern.

He figured it out anyway. "You still worried about what people will think?"

She nodded. "I have reasons—good reasons—for guarding our privacy."

"I take it Mom and Dad would not be thrilled to see you keeping company with the Hardison black sheep." He tried to sound cavalier about it, but she could tell just by the tone of his voice that he was bothered by this idea.

"Let's just say they wouldn't understand," she said. "Given what they know of my personality, they would worry if I suddenly took up with *anybody* at this stage in my life. I'm supposed to be focused on launching my career."

"You don't think they'd jump for joy if they discovered you were carousing with Jeff?"

Anne couldn't honestly answer no to that question. Her mother, especially, had always held a secret, not-too-well-disguised hope that Anne and Jeff would get married someday.

"Uh-huh, see?"

"They would worry no matter who it was," she insisted. "Especially if they knew we weren't just going to the movies. But I'm concerned about your family, too."

"Why? They already think I'm bad news. If anything, having you on my arm would elevate their opinion of me."

"No, no, you've got it wrong. I'm like a sister, a daughter, a granddaughter to the whole lot of them. If you never want to make peace with them, just tell them you're sleeping with me, commitment-free."

She didn't add that Jeff, in particular, wouldn't be pleased that Anne couldn't find time for him but could for his brother. Jeff had been so good to her over the years, but especially recently. She had no desire to hurt him.

What it boiled down to, though, was that she didn't want the whole world to know Wade was the father of the child she'd lost. If she and Wade became an item, speculation would run rampant. The Cottonwood grapevine would strike again. Anne wasn't sure how his family would judge him for fathering a child out of wedlock, but they might assume the worst—that he'd been deliberately irresponsible with a girl he hardly knew, then had abandoned her.

Wade sighed. "I guess I see your point. Neither of us needs any extra grief from the kinfolk. Tell you what. You can meet me at the old barn, like the other night," he suggested. "It's a big ranch. We'll ride away from the cows, through the trees. No one will even know we're there."

She nodded slowly. A secret affair. She, Anne Chatsworth, was having a secret, sordid affair. The realization should have been shocking. Instead it gave her a little thrill.

"Tomorrow?" he prodded.

"Tuesday. I've got an out-of-town job interview tomorrow."

"Tuesday. And wear some more of that sexy underwear."

In the truck on the way back to Antonio's parking lot, Anne found a brush in her purse and restored order to her hair, then pulled it back with an elastic. With some lotion and a tissue she removed the mascara that had smeared under her eyes, then applied some clear lip gloss.

Funny, though. When she checked her appearance in the rearview mirror, she still looked like Annie. She supposed Annie had more to do with attitude than makeup and hair. And she supposed Wade was right—Annie was a part of her, not some made-up personality.

Chapter Seven

When Anne got home, there was no avoiding her mother, who was lurking by the back door when Anne entered.

If Deborah had looked surprised by Anne's appearance earlier that day, she looked downright shocked now. "Anne Chatsworth, what have you been up to?"

"I can't answer that." Anne slid past her mother to the kitchen, where she poured herself a glass of water.

"What do you mean? You've always told me everything." She seemed more hurt than angry, and Anne felt a surge of guilt. She and her mother had always been close. When Anne had discovered she was pregnant, Deborah had been the first person she'd told. And after crying for half an hour, her mother had responded with love and sympathy, never condemnation.

But she just couldn't tell her mother about Wade.

Anne put down her water glass and hugged her mother. "Mom. I'm twenty-five years old. I have a personal life, and it's not something I can talk about right now."

"You worry me."

"I'm just letting off a little steam."

"But that's what you said you were doing when you...when you..."

When she accidentally got pregnant. Darn, she shouldn't have mentioned steam.

"You're having sex," Deborah concluded.

Anne couldn't very well deny it. "I'm being careful."

"That's not the point. Anne, this just isn't like you."

"Maybe it's exactly like me," she retorted, thinking of Annie. "There's a whole side to my personality you don't even know."

"And I'm not sure I want to. I saw those underthings you have hanging in the bathroom. Really, darling."

Anne paused, got hold of her temper. Her mother was only trying to protect her, guide her, help her make intelligent decisions, just the way she'd done Anne's whole life. But Anne was grown now. She had to make her own mistakes.

"I'm sorry, Mom. I know you want what's best for me. But there are some things I just have to do. I would never be able to explain them to you, so please don't ask me to. I'm not doing anything illegal or dangerous. And good heavens, there's nothing wrong with wearing sexy underwear. You should try it sometime."

Deborah looked scandalized. "Good Lord, what a suggestion." But then she forced a smile. "All right,

Anne. Sometimes I forget you're grown-up. Sometimes I forget what it was like to be young. You're not in love, are you?''

''Absolutely not,'' Anne answered too quickly. Love? No, no way. She couldn't be. Obsessed, maybe, but not in love.

''Good, I think. Love can really mess up your life.''

''Thank you, Mom.''

As Anne headed for the stairs, intending to take a shower, her mother offered one final caution. ''I'd be careful where your father's concerned. He's a bit more bullheaded than me, and if he'd seen you today, either before or after your lunch date, he would have interrogated you like you were a hostile witness.''

That, Anne was afraid, was the truth. She was still determined not to lie to either of her parents, but that didn't mean she had to throw her objectionable behavior in their faces. She would be careful, as her mother had warned.

ANNE TRIED REALLY HARD to concentrate on her studies. Fortunately she had a job interview in Dallas on Monday, the day after her picnic with Wade, which occupied most of her time. The job was with a huge firm that occupied three floors of a downtown skyscraper.

Dallas was familiar, and if she worked here she was only a three-hour drive from her parents. She also caught herself thinking she wouldn't be so far from Wade's home base. If he succeeded in mending fences with his family, he might spend more time in Cottonwood.

She wasn't actually considering a long-distance relationship with Wade, was she? He'd said they could manage it if they worked hard enough. He'd really gone out on a limb by admitting he wanted more than a casual affair. And while that proposition held incredible appeal, she had not reciprocated with any similar declarations.

It just wasn't possible. Long-distance relationships never worked. And, anyway, if she spent too much time mooning about an absent boyfriend, it would be career suicide.

Fortunately, this wasn't a decision she had to make. She hated the Dallas firm on sight. The offices were boring, generic. Everyone seemed to be dressed in the same suit. No one smiled. No one laughed. She felt the interview went well and that she presented herself with intelligence and professionalism. But her responsibilities, should she take the job, sounded like pure drudgery.

She'd been prepared for the life of a first-year lawyer at a large firm. She knew it was hard work and far from glamorous, that the closest she would get to a courtroom might be to do research for one of the more senior attorneys trying a case. She was prepared for hard work, but she at least wanted to be at a firm where she was more than a robot.

The offer was on the table. Anne could have this job if she wanted it. She told them she would be in touch, and got out of there before she did something very inappropriate, like laugh.

Maybe a smaller firm. Small but prestigious, where she stood a chance of making partner in something less than twenty years. Where her contributions would be noticed and appreciated. Where she could make a difference.

Wow, now *that* was an idealistic thought. Most law students got over that wide-eyed, crusader-lawyer image in their first year. In real life, practicing law was about making money and creating security. No matter what the economy, people always needed lawyers.

Anne had never been idealistic, because her father hadn't allowed it. So why now, of all times, did she catch herself wanting to "make a difference"?

Something to ponder.

As Tuesday rolled around, Anne found it harder to focus on books and jobs and letters of recommendation. She would see Wade again soon, and she'd run out of excuses. She really had to tell him about the baby this time. Which meant this might very well be their last time together.

She could admit now that she wanted to seize what pleasure she could, while she could. In a very short time, her life would no longer be her own, and her memories of her time with Wade would have to sustain her through some long, lonely months, maybe years. But anything long-term just wasn't feasible, no matter how they might want it.

Are you sure about that? her inner voice taunted her.

"Yes," she said aloud. It was a matter of making choices, setting priorities and looking at repercussions. Her father had always taught her that she could have anything she wanted if she put her mind to it. But that definitely didn't mean she could have *everything* she wanted.

WADE GOT UP from the kitchen table to get the mustard for his ham sandwich, then rustled around in the refrigerator looking for leftover new potatoes from last night. When he couldn't find them, he went to the pantry for the potato chips, then remembered that Jonathan didn't want Kristin to have potato chips for every meal.

He sat down, started to put mustard on his bread, then decided he needed a glass of milk.

"You're jumpy as a cat with fleas," Jonathan commented. "Something bothering you?"

"No, not a thing." Except Anne was due to arrive in a few minutes at the old barn, and Wade was anxious to saddle a couple of horses and meet her down there.

"Kristin," Jonathan said, "you're not eating."

"I'm not hungry," she said, picking at the crusts of her untouched peanut-butter-and-jelly sandwich.

Both Jonathan and Wade stopped what they were doing and stared. Kristin was always hungry. She was a regular little Mexican jumping bean, and she needed a lot of fuel.

Jonathan felt her forehead. "Do you feel okay, punkin'?"

"I can't breathe very good."

"Oh, great, she's probably caught Pete's cold," Jonathan said as he got up to find the thermometer. Pete had awakened the day after his birthday party sneezing and coughing like an old steam engine. He'd taken to his bed, and Wade had been taking him his meals on a tray.

Sally had dropped by more than once, too, seeming to delight in caring for the grumpy old bird.

Jonathan located the thermometer and stuck it in Kristin's ear. She didn't protest, didn't even wiggle, and Wade realized she did seem a bit listless.

"She's running a little fever," Jonathan said.

"I'm not sick," Kristin insisted.

"Sounds like you have the sniffles, though," Jonathan said.

"Can I still ride Misty?" she asked in alarm. Kristin was definitely her father's daughter. She could ride her pony better than most weathered ranch hands handled their mounts, and she lived in blue jeans and boots.

"I think you better stick around here and rest," Jonathan said.

"But, Daddy, you promised!" Kristin screeched.

"You can't go riding if you're sick," Jonathan reasoned, though Wade knew from experience that Kristin hadn't yet achieved the age of reason. "We'll go as soon as you're all well."

"I want to go *now!*"

Jonathan pinched the bridge of his nose. "Don't you want to stay here and watch cartoons with Uncle Wade?"

"No, I want to ride Misty!" With that she launched herself into a full-scale tantrum, forcing both men to cover their ears.

"I hate to do this to you," Jonathan said to Wade over the ruckus, "but do you mind keeping an eye on her this afternoon?"

Ordinarily, Wade wouldn't have minded at all. Even Kristin's tantrum didn't faze him—he considered it a challenge to woo her out of it. But he didn't consider responsibility for a five-year-old conducive to the romantic afternoon he had planned with Anne.

"What?" Jonathan asked, apparently reading the hesitation in Wade's face. "You have plans?"

"I sort of thought I might take Cimmy out and put her through her paces." Cimmaron, Cimmy for short, was the black mare Jonathan had offered Wade as a replacement for Traveler. Wade had planned to ride her on his and Anne's outing. Traveler wasn't exactly rocketing to recovery, and Wade figured he ought to at least think about training another horse. It was too late for this year, and it would mean another full year of competition before he could retire, but that was life.

At least Jonathan looked pleased that Wade had taken an interest in the mare. "If I come back early, you'll still have a couple of hours of daylight."

Wade shrugged. "Sure. I'll watch the bedbug." What choice did he have? If he wanted to be a member of his family, and not just a barely tolerated interloper, he had to take some responsibility.

"I'm not a bedbug," Kristin said.

Wade feigned surprise. "You're not? Oh, my gosh, you're right. You're a cute little girl."

"I'm not, either. I'm a cowgirl!" Kristin burst into tears again, and Wade shrugged. He'd tried.

Jonathan took his dishes to the sink, smiling wryly. "Did you take Pete his lunch?"

"He was still asleep when I checked."

"That's good. He didn't sleep so well last night."

"I'll make sure he eats something when he wakes up." Wade pulled Kristin into his lap and cuddled her, then blew her nose with a paper napkin. Her tantrum was already winding down.

"I'll be back around four." Jonathan donned his hat, kissed a resistant Kristin on the cheek and took off out the back door. No sooner was he gone than Wade grabbed the phone and dialed Anne's cell number. She'd given it to him before they'd parted on Sunday, explaining that was the easiest, most discreet method of reaching her.

"Anne Chatsworth," she answered in her lawyer voice.

"Hey, lawyer-babe, it's your big boy."

"Wade! You embarrass me to pieces." He could hear the roar of her Mustang in the background and realized she was already on her way over.

"I got bad news, darlin'. I drew baby-sitting duty. Kristin's got a cold, Pete's sick..."

"I'm not a baby," Kristin insisted again, though not as emphatically as before. She stuck her thumb in her mouth, a sure sign she was getting sleepy.

"I'm sorry as he—" Wade quickly censored himself "—as heck."

"That's okay," Anne said. "We can get together another day. I wouldn't want you to duck out of baby-sitting just for me." The disappointment in her voice mirrored his own. Sure, they could meet some other time, but how much time did they have left? Only a couple of weeks before he and Traveler were headed for Kansas City. And she'd probably be gone by the time he came back.

"Can't a body get anything to eat around here?" Pete's cough-roughened voice berated from the hallway. He leaned heavily on his cane as he entered the kitchen. He hadn't bothered putting a robe over his ratty old flannel pajamas.

"Um, let me call you back in a few," Wade quickly said to Anne. "We might not have to postpone our business after all."

The old man scowled. "Who was that?"

"Nobody important. What would you like to eat?" Wade asked, hoping to forestall any nosy questions. "Soup and a ham sandwich okay?"

"Yeah, whatever. I'll eat in the den." Pete looked at Kristin. "What's wrong with her?"

"Sniffles," Wade answered.

His grandfather looked horrified. "Did I give the doodlebug my cold?"

"There's lots of germs milling around these days," Wade said. "You probably both caught the same bug from someone at the party."

Pete grumbled as he headed for his recliner in the den. Wade put Kristin down for her nap—she went without a whimper—then quickly made a sandwich and microwaved some soup. He put the food and a glass of milk on a tray, which he took to Pete, who was ensconced in his recliner with a rainbow-hued afghan covering his sinewy frame. He was watching a cooking show, of all things.

"How you feeling, Granddad?" Wade asked, carefully setting the tray over his grandfather's lap.

"Like hob. But I guess I'll survive."

"Your cough sounds better."

"That's 'cause I took the cure. Works every time."

"Good. I was thinking about going for a ride, working with that black mare of Jon's. Would you mind watching Kristin for a couple of hours? She's napping, and she might not even wake up."

"'Course I'll watch her. Don't I every day of my life?"

"I just thought, since you're under the weather—"

"The day I'm too sick to watch my great-granddaughter, shoot me. Now go take your ride."

Wade grinned. "Thanks."

He dialed Anne's number again as he pulled on his boots. "Change of plans," he said. "Are you still free?"

"I was driving around waiting to hear from you."

"I'll meet you at the old barn in fifteen minutes."

"I'll be there."

ANNE'S BODY WAS PRIMED. She'd been reliving her and Wade's encounter by the creek ever since it had happened, counting the hours until they could be together again. When he'd called to cancel, she'd been disappointed all out of proportion, her body all full of hormones that would now serve no useful purpose. Then, when he'd called again, she'd pulled a U-turn in the middle of the highway and headed back toward the Hardison Ranch, every cell in her body jumping.

She knew they'd make love again. She'd decided she could handle it, one more time. Then she would tell him her secret. If he was angry, if he told her to get out of his life and stay gone this time, she was prepared.

Oh, shoot, who was she trying to fool? If he kicked her out of his life, she would be devastated. But she wouldn't blame him if that was exactly what he did. And she couldn't be deterred by his possible reaction.

"I can tell him now," she reminded herself, "or he could find out from someone else."

She parked her car near some bushes, where it couldn't be seen from either the street or the house, then slipped inside the cavernous barn with an armload of books.

"Wade?"

No answer. Anne got an apprehensive flutter in her stomach. When she'd first moved to Cottonwood, she'd gotten set up by some cruel girls who'd told her to meet them at a boarded-up house so she could join their club. When she'd arrived, thinking that at last she would have some friends, only silence had greeted her. When she came back out of the house, her bike had been stolen.

She never approached any meeting without thinking about that incident, especially when she had to wait.

Fortunately, after a couple of minutes she heard the pounding of horse hooves approaching. She peeked outside and saw Wade riding a magnificent black horse, leading a smaller, fatter horse.

"Sorry I'm late," Wade said, swinging down from the black. "This devil-horse didn't want to be caught. I had to chase her around the pasture and lasso her."

"I thought you were supposed to rope the calves, not the horses." Anne steered clear of the intimidating black horse, but she petted the other one, which seemed docile enough.

Wade took a coil of rope off his horse's saddle. "I rope whatever's trying to move faster than me." He casually tossed the rope toward her, and before she could blink, the lasso was tight around her shoulders.

Wade reeled her in as she laughed and tried to struggle free.

"Hey, this is totally unnecessary," she protested. "It's not like I'm running from you." Not at the moment, anyway.

"Better not." He kissed her, fast and hard, then released her.

"How's Kristin?" she asked

"She was napping when I left. She was running a little fever, but I think she'll be fine."

"Does Rita ever see them?" Anne remembered Jonathan's ex-wife as beautiful but very reserved, perpetually frowning. She'd never warmed up to Anne's attempts at friendship.

"Just holidays and a couple of weeks in the summer. She lives in New Orleans, and she claims to believe the ranch is a better environment for growing kids than the city. Personally I think she just doesn't want to be bothered."

Anne gave a little shiver. "I can't imagine bearing children and then giving them up…" Her face grew hot as she realized what she'd just said. She couldn't imagine willingly turning her back on her own flesh and blood, but she knew exactly how it felt to be forced to give one up.

A single tear had escaped her right eye and trickled down her cheek. She turned to pet the chubby brown horse again, hoping Wade wouldn't notice as she surreptitiously rubbed her eye.

"Anne? Are you *crying?*"

Damn. "It just strikes me as being sad, that's all. Children should have a full-time mother." And a father. But she'd planned to raise hers without one of those. Quite a double standard.

Wade came over and slid his arms around her. "That's sweet. Didn't know you were such a sentimental softy."

She relaxed into his light embrace, absorbing comfort she didn't deserve.

"Are you sure you're cut out to be a tough, kick-ass lawyer?"

"I have to have empathy for my clients, don't I? When a person seeks out a lawyer, they're usually in some kind of difficulty. Understanding how they feel will make me a better advocate, will help me to—"

"Anne, I wasn't serious. I know you'll be an excellent lawyer."

"Even if my being a lawyer takes me away from here?" *Away from you?*

He nodded. "You'd be unhappy if you weren't doing what you were meant to do. That was Rita's problem, I think. They really did love each other, from what hints Jonathan has dropped. But she was a city girl through and through, educated and primed for a career in high finance. She gave it all up to be a ranch wife, and that was a mistake."

"Maybe so, but a commitment is a commitment. I didn't know her very well, and maybe I shouldn't judge, but it doesn't seem like running away from your own family is the right answer."

Again Anne realized she'd put her foot in her mouth.

Fortunately, Wade didn't take offense. "It isn't. I learned that lesson the hard way." He tethered the horses to a tree, where they immediately began munching the thick, unmown grass. "Bring your books?"

"You bet. They're in the barn."

"I thought we could study for a while," he said, "then take our ride."

"Sounds reasonable." She was surprised he took her studying so seriously. She'd half expected him to wiggle out of his responsibilities. Then again, maybe he'd only intended to lure her to the hayloft, which was the only place in the barn bright enough to study. But apparently he didn't have seduction in mind. He settled on the hay a healthy distance from her and asked how he could be most helpful.

"You can ask me questions out of this bar review book," she said, handing him a paperback the size of a Sears catalogue.

He did, but Anne had a terrible time focusing on her studies with Wade so near, lounging like a tomcat, looking big and male and touchable in his jeans and flannel shirt. She realized she'd never seen him wearing anything but jeans and couldn't imagine him in any other clothes.

What if she took him to an office get-together, after she accepted a position with a law firm? Did he own a tie?

"Anne? How long are you going to take to answer that one?"

Anne realized she hadn't heard a word of the sample question Wade had asked her from the preparation book. She shook her head to clear it. "I'm sorry, my mind wandered."

"Yeah, to something pretty disturbing if that frown is any indication. What were you thinking about?"

About how impossible it is for us to be together. Anne forced a laugh. ''Nothing important. Would you repeat the question?''

Wade shook his head. ''We've been at this for an hour and a half.''

''That's not really very long.'' She'd been known to study for five or six hours on end without taking a break.

''It is for me. You need some fresh air to clear the fog out of your brain. And those horses are getting pretty restless. I hear 'em stomping and snorting down there.'' He got up and dragged Anne with him. ''Come on, lawyer-girl, let's go ride some ponies.''

Uneasiness of a whole different kind assaulted her. ''I'm not sure I want to—''

''Yes, you do. I won't let anything happen to you, I promise.''

Oddly enough, she totally believed him.

Anne put her books in the trunk of her car, then swallowed her fear as she returned to the horses and tried not to let them intimidate her. She'd heard horses could smell fear.

''This is Danny. He's Sam's new horse. Sam's outgrown his pony.''

''Little Sam rides this monster?''

''He's just now learning. Another couple of months, and maybe a growth spurt, and they'll be a perfect match. Danny's ten years old and gentle as a lamb.'' Wade tightened the girth, then helped Anne to mount. The horse stood patiently, waiting for Anne to put her right foot in the stirrup.

''Who's the other horse?'' she asked. ''He's gorgeous.''

"She. Cimmaron. Jonathan wants to give her to me, sort of a peace offering."

"That's a pretty generous gesture. Are you accepting?"

"I don't know," Wade said, tightening his own horse's cinch. "I've never competed with any horse but Traveler, not since I was a kid. It seems disloyal."

"I'm sure Traveler wouldn't mind sharing the limelight. Maybe he'd like a rest now and then. How's he doing, anyway?"

"He's walking a little better today, and he was getting really anxious cooped up in that stall, so I let him out in the pasture."

"That's a good sign, huh?"

"Yeah. There's still a chance I can ride him at the Royal. And if not..."

"There's Cimmaron."

"Cimmy probably won't be ready by then, either. She needs a lot of work."

"So you might as well get started."

"Yeah," he said on a sigh. "I guess she deserves a chance."

Anne's heart went out to Wade. His loyalty to Traveler, though not entirely practical, was admirable. A man that loyal would never abandon his children....

Oh, why did her thoughts always stray in that direction? Wade and children. Wade and family. Wade and babies. She had to stop thinking about that. Besides, he wasn't some paragon of loyalty. He'd run away from home at sixteen, after all.

But he's trying to make amends for that now, she reminded herself. A man who could admit mistakes wasn't such a bad deal, either. And if she wasn't careful, she would be nominating Wade for sainthood.

Wade reminded her how to hold the reins and how to position her legs and feet. She felt as if she was a hundred feet off the ground, but Danny stood still as a statue for her, which was somewhat reassuring.

Wade swung up on Cimmy, who pranced and snorted dramatically, and they were off.

After a few minutes Anne started to relax. She practiced starting and stopping and turning, and she was amazed that she felt confident enough to urge Danny into a trot, then an easy canter, at least for a few strides.

"You're getting the hang of it," Wade encouraged.

"I can see why this appeals to you so much," she said, grinning at her accomplishments. "It's like...I don't know, like the horse is an extension of me, at least when I'm doing everything right and we're communicating."

"I'll turn you into a cowgirl yet."

"Wouldn't those 4-H kids be surprised. My dad wouldn't buy me a calf or a horse or a pig or anything. I finally talked him into a few chickens, but I had to keep them at someone else's farm because the ordinances at the lake wouldn't allow it."

"But I bet you raised some fine chickens."

"Wrong. I entered my best rooster in one show, and the scrawny thing was such an embarrassment I never did it again."

"Poor Anne. You can take the girl out of the city..."

"Hey, there's hope for me. I'm riding a horse, aren't I?"

"And doing very well."

His praise pleased her out of all proportion. What did it matter whether she could play at being a cowgirl? Ranches and rodeos were not ever going to be a significant aspect of her life. After all, how many cowboys needed a lawyer?

They rode through fields and woods, across creeks, then right through the middle of a herd of brown-and-white cows. Herefords? Maybe. She really didn't remember much of what she'd learned in 4-H. After forty-five minutes, Anne's backside started to tingle, and she realized she was going to be sore tomorrow.

She kept hoping Wade would suggest they stop and dismount, maybe walk a few minutes. Maybe sit under a tree. Or lie in the grass. But he didn't. He seemed pretty intent on putting the shiny black horse through her paces, making tight circles around bushes, cutting a bewildered cow from the herd, stopping on a dime, then racing across a field as fast as she would go. By the time they turned back toward the barn, Cimmy was lathered and Wade was breathless but exhilarated.

"So?" Anne asked. "Good calf-roping material?"

He nodded. "Real good. Better than I expected." He reached forward to pat Cimmy's neck. Just then a butterfly fluttered up and landed on the mare's nose. She rolled her eyes back, whinnied in panic, and reared up on her hind legs, then bucked, dumping Wade unceremoniously onto the ground. Free of her rider, she took off at a dead run toward the barn, which wasn't far off.

"Wade! Are you hurt?" Anne hurriedly, clumsily dismounted, but Wade was already sitting up, laughing.

"She's real good except for *that.* How humiliating. I haven't had a horse dump me since I gave up bronc riding at eighteen."

Anne offered him a hand and helped him to his feet. "That's okay. We all need a lesson in humility now and then."

They held hands and walked the rest of the way to the barn, leading a docile Danny behind. Anne tried not to feel too disappointed that Wade hadn't wanted to make love to her while they were out. It was better this way. She should not be making love to a man she was deceiving.

As they neared the barn, the sound of a siren penetrated Anne's consciousness. Wade heard it, too. He stopped and stared into the distance.

"Wonder what that's all about?"

They started walking again, but the siren got louder. Pretty soon flashing lights were visible through the tree line that bordered the road in front of the house.

"It's coming this way," Anne said, looking around for telltale smoke from a fire. Then the ambulance turned into the Hardison driveway.

Wade cursed and took off at a dead run toward the house.

Chapter Eight

Wade ran flat-out all the way to the back door, arriving about the same time the paramedics were barging through the front. Had something happened to Pete? Kristin knew enough to call 9-1-1 if someone was sick or hurt.

Wade headed for the living room, meeting Pete and the paramedics at the same time. His relief at seeing Pete conscious and running around was quickly doused by the realization that if it wasn't Pete who was sick…

Oh, God, no.

"This way," Pete told the paramedics, motioning for them to follow him toward the bedrooms.

Wade followed on their heels, and the sight that met him in Kristin's bedroom turned his blood to ice water. Kristin lay on the carpet near her bed, surrounded by a halo of bright red.

"What's her name?" one of the paramedics asked as he checked the little girl's condition.

"Kristin," Pete answered. "Last I knew she was napping. I was watching TV—I guess I must have dozed off. Then I heard this big crash—"

"Kristin? Can you hear me?" the paramedic asked.

Kristin didn't move, didn't speak, didn't cry. She remained alarmingly still.

Working with quiet efficiency, though with a sense of urgency, the paramedics put Kristin on a backboard, then a stretcher. They wrapped her head in gauze, and only then did Wade get a glimpse of the source of all that blood—a gash on the side of Kristin's head. A splash of bright crimson decorated the nightstand. It appeared she had fallen somehow and struck her head.

"Did you call Jonathan?" Wade asked Pete.

He nodded, looking suddenly old to Wade. "Got him on the cell phone. He should be here any minute."

Wade backed into the hallway to give the paramedics room to wheel Kristin out. It was all happening so quickly, like a nightmare on fast-forward.

He realized Anne was there beside him, watching the proceedings with her arms tightly crossed, her face paper-white.

"What happened?" she asked.

"We don't know. Looks like she hit her head."

"We'll take her to Mother Frances Hospital in Tyler," one of the paramedics said over his shoulder as they wheeled Kristin out the front door to the waiting ambulance. "They have a level-1 trauma unit and a neurosurgeon on call."

Trauma...neurosurgeon...

"I'm sorry," Pete said to no one in particular.

"I'm sure it wasn't your fault," Anne said, giving Pete's shoulders a quick squeeze.

Pete only then noticed her. "Anne? What in tarnation are you doing here?"

"Ah, long story. What can I do to help? Should I stay here and wait for Jonathan?"

"I'll stay," Pete said. "Got to put on some clothes, anyway, before I go anywhere."

"I'm going to the hospital," Wade said.

"I'll drive you if you want," Anne offered.

Wade appreciated her offer more than he could say. He didn't want to take the time to unhitch his trailer from his truck. Wade was also immeasurably grateful for Anne's calming presence during the interminable drive to Tyler. He was as close to falling apart as he'd ever been.

"I can't believe this," he kept saying. "How could this happen?"

Anne had no answers for him. She just silently reached over and placed her hand over his. At least she didn't mouth any meaningless platitudes, like *She'll be fine* or *God will take care of her.* Kristin had been unconscious, probably for several minutes. He'd been witness to enough rodeo accidents to know what prolonged unconsciousness could mean.

It took a grueling forty-five minutes to get to Tyler, even with Anne pushing the Mustang past eighty. She grabbed the first parking place she came to, then they literally sprinted to the emergency room, only to find out their haste was useless. No one could tell them anything about Kristin's condition, other than, "Doctors are with her now, and we'll let you know as soon as we have any news."

Wade tried to answer some questions about Kristin, but he quickly discovered how little he knew about his niece. He knew nothing about her medical history, her insurance, her allergies. He wasn't even 100 percent sure of her birthday.

"Her father should be here shortly," Wade finally said. "He'll know all this stuff."

Almost before the words were out of his mouth, Jonathan burst through the E.R. doors, a bundle of barely contained fury. "Where is she?" he demanded. "What the hell happened?"

"She's with the doctors now," Wade said, unable to imagine the horror his brother must be going through.

Jonathan turned his wrath on the poor woman at the information desk, threatening to climb over whoever or whatever stood between himself and his daughter. Wade knew he ought to do something to calm his brother down, to reassure him everything possible was being done for Kristin. But they hadn't been close in so long—hell, with seven years between them, they'd never been real close.

Maybe this was the time to change that. He laid a soothing hand on Jonathan's arm. "Come sit down, Jon."

Jonathan tensed at the physical contact, and the look he shot Wade could have boiled oil. "Don't touch me. What are you doing here, anyway? Haven't you done enough?"

Wade shrank back at his brother's acid tone and the burning accusation in his eyes. "I'm here to help."

"Like you did earlier? I entrusted my sick daughter's care to you. And what did you do? You abdicated responsibility—typical. You left her alone with a sick, drunk old man who can't even take care of himself—"

"Granddad was not drunk!" Wade shot back. "He was awake and watching TV when I left—"

"Please, spare me the excuses. I don't want you to ever come near either of my children again."

"Jonathan," Anne said. "Don't say things you might regret later."

Startled, Jonathan noticed Anne for the first time. "Where'd you come from?"

"I was with Wade," she said without hesitation—something else for Wade to appreciate. He knew how important it was for Anne to protect her privacy, and she'd just thrown that down the drain, all because she thought she might be of some help.

Jonathan narrowed his eyes. "*With* Wade?"

"He was helping me study, and then we went riding," she said, raising her chin a notch, daring him to challenge her.

Instead he turned back to Wade, shock in his expression. "She's the one you were mooning about the other day? The one you…in the barn?" Before Wade could even respond, Jonathan turned back to Anne. "I'm disappointed in you. I thought you had more sense than that."

Anne blanched at the unprovoked attack. She actually took a step back. She opened her mouth to retort, but she never got the chance. Jeff's arrival redirected Jonathan's focus. He turned to greet his other brother, and it was as if Wade and Anne had ceased to exist.

Wade took Anne's hand and led her to a remote corner of the waiting room. "Guess he let us know where we stand,'' he said as he sank into a chair, numb with the aftermath of Jonathan's anger.

''I'm sure he didn't mean it,'' Anne said. ''He's scared to death right now, and he's lashing out in fear. He wants to blame someone or something for what can only be called a senseless accident.''

''Yeah, well, I can see him getting mad at me, but I draw the line at what he said to you. If it wasn't his daughter back there with the doctors, I'd have—''

''Don't even think about it.'' Anne grabbed his clenched fist in her hands and forcefully uncurled his fingers.

''You can leave if you want,'' he said, though he hoped against hope she'd stay. He needed her. He'd never thought he would need anyone, but his heart had opened up these past couple of weeks. He'd learned to care again—about the kids, his brothers and the rest of the family, and about Anne. He'd forgotten, though, that caring could lead to hurting.

''I'll stay.'' She continued holding his hand.

Jeff and Jonathan conferred in hushed voices on the other side of the waiting room. Jeff cast a curious glance toward Wade and Anne every so often, and Wade could just imagine what was being said. Then both men disappeared through the door into the treatment area, Jeff's status as a doctor conferring special privileges.

''I probably ought to think about finding a new place to bunk,'' Wade said. ''Jonathan didn't really like me hanging around in the first place, but he tolerated me out of a sense of duty or something. Sounds like now he wants me gone.''

"Don't make any hasty decisions," Anne said. "He'll probably forget he ever said those things to you."

"Don't count on it. My brother has a memory like an elephant, especially when it comes to recalling my transgressions. And, hell, maybe he's right. He did leave Kristin in my care. He trusted me. And I foisted her off on Granddad when I knew he'd taken some of his special cough remedy."

"Codeine?" Anne asked.

Wade grimaced. "No, it's made from honey, lemon and whiskey. But he wasn't drunk."

"I can't imagine that he would be. I know Pete likes his Kentucky bourbon, but I've never seen him overdo it."

"Still, I shouldn't have left him alone with Kristin. But I was more concerned about my own selfish—"

"Wade, don't. Please don't blame yourself. There was nothing wrong with leaving Kristin in Pete's care for a couple of hours. He takes care of her all the time."

"Then why'd she get hurt?"

In answer, Anne reached up and parted her hair at a place above her left ear, revealing a small, jagged scar. "See that?"

He did. He also saw a lot of other things, like the way her hair glowed almost burgundy under the fluorescent waiting-room lights, and the graceful turn of her hand and the delicacy of her wrist. A lot of things he shouldn't be thinking about at a time like this.

"I got it when I was five," she said. "I was jumping on the couch, pretending I was Wonder Woman, and I fell off and hit the coffee table."

"You think that's what Kristin was doing? Jumping on the bed?"

"Or some other kind of horseplay. It just happened, and it would have happened if Dr. Spock himself had been baby-sitting. It's no one's fault, and Jonathan will realize that soon enough."

"I hope you're right. I can't imagine what he's going through." Wade stretched his legs out and crossed his ankles, trying to get comfortable in the granite-like waiting-room chair. "I've only known Kristin a couple of weeks, and it's ripping me up inside thinking I might lose her. But if I'd watched her being born, heard her first words and seen her take her first steps—I don't see how Jonathan can stand the pain."

Anne bowed her head. "It must be awful for him." Her voice was barely above a whisper.

ANNE ALMOST CAME UNGLUED, listening to Wade talk about being a father. If she'd had any idea of his feelings on this subject, she would have moved heaven and earth to locate him when she found out she was pregnant. The disservice—the downright insult—she'd done him by keeping the baby a secret was a crime.

She realized now there was no hope he would ever forgive her. She also realized she hadn't yet told him, despite her earlier promise to herself to do it. Well, she couldn't say anything about it now—that would be the heart of cruelty.

Unfortunately, she was very afraid Wade was right about Jonathan—he might not ever forgive Wade, illogical as such a grudge would be. She'd never seen such fury in anyone, least of all the normally placid, low-key Jonathan Hardison. Jonathan had been slow accepting Wade back into the family, and this supposed transgression would set Wade back where he started—the black-sheep brother.

Jeff returned to the waiting room a few minutes later without Jonathan. He gave Anne a hard look. She couldn't meet his gaze.

He sat down in the row of chairs opposite them. "How are you involved in this thing, Anne?"

"Anne and I went for a ride," Wade said.

Jeff looked confused. "Because..."

"Because it was a beautiful day. Do we need another reason?"

Understanding slowly dawned on Jeff's face. "I guess your busy schedule opened up unexpectedly, huh, Anne?"

"Jeff, don't do this. Now's not the time."

Wade looked from Anne to his brother and back again. "What are you talking about?"

This was exactly the reason she didn't want the whole world to know she and Wade were involved. She ignored Wade and focused on Jeff. "I didn't lie to you."

"You're obviously not as busy as you claimed." He cast another accusatory look at Wade.

"Oh, Jeff, grow up," Anne said in disgust, tired of all this walking on eggshells. "I know you're not used to any woman turning you down, but it happened, okay? It has nothing to do with Wade."

Wade interrupted. "Can you two talk about your love life later? I'd like to know how Kristin is doing. She'll be okay, won't she, Jeff?"

Jeff seemed to physically shake himself, then slide into his doctor persona. "They're taking her to surgery now. She's got a hematoma—"

"Talk English, please," Wade said impatiently. "Long, Latin words always sound scarier than ordinary ones."

"She's bleeding inside her head. They have to operate to relieve the pressure. Her CAT scan showed no obvious damage to the brain, and she has no other apparent injuries."

"Will she be okay?"

"There's a very good chance she'll be just fine, though any kind of surgery on the brain has its risks."

Anne allowed herself one full, deep breath. She was sure she'd been holding her breath since she'd first seen that ambulance.

"Wade, what happened?" Jeff answered. "I couldn't get a straight answer out of Jon—he just kept blaming you. And Pete just kept blubbering that it was all his fault."

"We don't know what happened, exactly. Kristin was napping, Pete was watching TV. He heard a loud noise and found her on the floor."

"And how is that your fault?" Jeff asked.

"I said I'd watch her. Then I didn't." He paused, looked away, his throat working furiously. "The more I think about it, the more justified Jonathan's anger becomes. He thinks I was ditching my responsibilities—like always."

Jeff shook his head sadly. "I expect he'll get over it." But he didn't sound that confident.

"It takes Jon a long time to get over things," Wade said, his own frustration coming to the surface. "I'm really tired of trying to prove myself to him every hour of every damn day. And frankly I'm not sure I can justify what happened—to him or to myself. I'm thinking I should leave the ranch.''

Anne found herself holding her breath yet again. He couldn't leave, not so soon. No matter how impossible a long-term relationship between the two of them was, she wanted the few days or weeks they had together.

''Don't run away,'' she said before she could think it through. Maybe this wasn't any of her business, but she couldn't keep silent. ''If you leave, you'll be admitting to Jonathan he was right. Stand your ground, or you'll never be a family again.''

''We haven't all been a family for a long time,'' Jeff said.

Wade stared at his brother a moment longer, obviously fighting the urge to argue. Then, abruptly, he stood. ''I'm going to find some coffee.'' He took off as if he was on a mission to save the world.

Anne didn't want to be alone with Jeff. His blue eyes, which could be so full of kindness and sympathy, also saw more than she was comfortable with. Right now he was treating her to a penetrating stare, which she tried to ignore.

He swiveled into the chair next to her and spoke in a low voice. ''You and Wade. I just don't get it.''

Anne did not want to have this conversation. She opened her purse, pulled out a nail file, and started working on her ragged fingernails.

''I know I told you to get back in the saddle,'' Jeff went on, ''but I didn't mean you should throw all your good sense out the window.''

"Meaning?" She knew exactly what he meant, but she wanted to make him say it.

"Wade isn't the sort of guy who..."

"Who what?"

"He's irresponsible. He's thoughtless. He'll take what he wants from you and dump you without a second thought. And that isn't the sort of treatment you need in your life right now."

Anne couldn't believe Jeff would talk about his own brother that way. "On what evidence do you base those conclusions?" she asked in her best almost-lawyer voice.

Jeff shrugged, as if the answer were obvious. "Because he's my brother. I know him."

"Do you? He's been back in Cottonwood for, what, two weeks?"

"About that."

"And how much time have you spent with him during those two weeks?"

"Not that much. He keeps to himself a lot. He'd rather spend time with his horse than his family."

"How much?" Anne persisted. "Five hours? Ten?"

"I don't appreciate being cross-examined, counselor."

"I'm just trying to figure out how you arrived at such a low opinion of your brother, when you haven't seen him since he was sixteen."

"Look, he turned his back on his own family for thirteen years. What kind of person does that? You can draw your own conclusions."

"I have. But they're based on what I see now, not what happened thirteen years ago. Wade has grown up into a good, decent person. He sees that he made a mistake, and he's trying to fix it. But the Hardisons just aren't a real forgiving lot of people."

"Why should we bother?" Jeff wanted to know. "He's just going to leave again, once his horse is better. You do realize that, don't you?"

"Of course. We've talked about it. But just because someone isn't physically present in your life all the time is no reason to shun them for eternity. I'm getting ready to move far away from my parents, because that's where my goals in life are leading me. That doesn't mean they'll stop loving me. On the contrary, they support me a hundred percent, because they want me to be happy."

"They wouldn't be so happy about you seeing Wade."

"No, they won't be," she agreed. Score a point for Jeff. "But they won't stop loving me for that, either."

"I don't want to be the one to have to pick up the pieces when Wade does a number on you," Jeff insisted. "He isn't right for you."

"Then who would be right for Anne?" Wade's voice interrupted. "You?"

Anne gasped. She and Jeff had been so engrossed in their argument neither of them had heard Wade returning. He stood before them clutching a foam cup of hot coffee, and for a moment Anne thought he might dump the coffee right on his brother.

Jeff at least had the good grace to look chagrined. He started to stumble through some explanation, but Wade cut him off. "I knew Jonathan had a chip on his shoulder where I'm concerned, just because I don't want to work on his damn ranch, but I thought

I could count on support from you. Hell, I guess you're like the rest of them. You wish I'd never come back.''

''Don't go reading things into a conversation you weren't supposed to hear,'' Jeff said. ''This has more to do with Anne than you. She's like a little sister to me, and she's very fragile right now.''

Anne gave Jeff a sharp look. He certainly hadn't been behaving in a brotherly fashion, not lately. And he'd better not say anything else referring to her fragile state or he'd be crossing that line of patient confidentiality.

He met her gaze, then nodded slightly, as if to say he understood.

''Why does everyone seem to think Anne needs protecting?'' Wade asked. ''It seems to me she's pretty good at taking care of herself.''

''I certainly can,'' Anne inserted smoothly. ''I get enough grief from my parents trying to run my life. Jeff, I appreciate your concern, but please butt out.''

Jeff looked at her for a moment as if he couldn't believe what she'd just said, then laughed, easing the tension slightly. ''Understood.''

''On that note I really should go,'' Anne said, realizing she should extricate herself now from what should be a private family crisis, now that her help wasn't needed. She didn't want to invite any further scrutiny about her and Wade—especially from Jeff, who might put two and two together. And she certainly didn't want to cause further friction within Wade's family.

Wade walked her out to her car. ''Sorry the afternoon turned out like it did.''

"Me, too. Will you call me and let me know how Kristin's surgery goes?"

He nodded.

"Why would Jeff assume you're going to dump me?" she asked.

Wade shrugged. "He has preconceived notions about rodeo cowboys. I guess he assumes you're just another of my supposed long list of conquests, another notch on my belt buckle."

Anne smiled at that notion. No matter how transitory their relationship, Wade had never made her feel she was just one in a vast sea of women in his life. He'd always been honest with her. She wished she could say the same of herself.

"I'm not sure how I got this reputation as a Romeo," Wade said.

"I seem to recall you had girls hanging all over you when you were sixteen," Anne said. "There was something very attractive about all that quiet seething. You seemed very dark and mysterious...and maybe a little dangerous."

"I was a lot more interested in horses than girls back then."

"And now?"

"I've learned a thing or two. Like, a horse can't keep you warm at night." He smiled and caressed her cheek with the tip of his finger. "I'd ask you to stay here with me, but I know you've got studying to do."

"The studying's not that important," she said, realizing for the first time that it really wasn't. What were a few more points on the bar exam when compared to the life of a little girl? "I just don't want to complicate matters by sticking around. People are bound to ask more questions, and I have no idea what to answer."

"You could tell them the truth."

"And what would that be?"

He flashed that adorable crooked smile of his. "That you're crazy about me."

"I think I'm just crazy, period. You're not really leaving the ranch, are you?"

He leaned in and gave her a quick but intense kiss, then turned and loped back toward the hospital. A little piece of her heart went with him.

Before returning home, Anne had to stop at the Hardison Ranch. She was worried about the horses, which she and Wade had abandoned.

She went to the old barn first, but there was no sign of either horse. So she walked up to the new barn and finally located them. Both were grazing in the small, adjacent pasture, their saddles and bridles gone. Someone had seen to their care.

She was about to return to her car and head home when she heard a funny sound coming from inside the barn, very faint. An animal in pain? She followed the sound and realized it was not an animal, but a child. She found Sam in the stall where Frogville was, curled up in a corner and crying his eyes out.

Poor little guy. "Sam?"

He looked up, then turned away, obviously embarrassed to be found acting like a baby.

Anne sat on the concrete floor next to him. "Want to talk about it?"

Chapter Nine

Sam looked at her earnestly, his big brown eyes reflecting fear no child should know. "Is my sister gonna die like Mike Uberhauser?"

"Who's Mike Uberhauser?" Anne asked, delaying her answer to the most difficult question anyone had ever asked her. Obviously, Sam had been told of the accident, but apparently no one had time to worry about how it would affect him.

"A kid in my class. He died last year 'cause he had leukemia. My teacher said he went to heaven. Will Kristin go to heaven?"

"If Kristin were to die, she most certainly would go to heaven, because she is a very good little girl. But we don't think she's going to die, not for years and years. She did get hurt, and she has to have an operation on her head, but the doctors are going to fix her up." Anne sent up a silent prayer that she was right.

"Can I go see her?"

"Not today. But maybe tomorrow." His little face fell, and Anne racked her brain for something to distract him. "Hey, I know. Why don't you get some crayons and draw a picture for Kristin? You can take it to her when you visit, and she can hang it on the wall in her hospital room. Then every time she sees it, even if you're not there she'll think of you."

Her suggestion seemed to appeal to Sam. At least he'd stopped crying. "What should I draw?"

"How about a picture of Alexander and Miss Pooh?"

Sam smiled. "And the ants. I've been feeding ants to 'em. They eat a lot."

Anne got up, took Sam's hand and walked him back up to the house, then helped him find paper and crayons. She fixed him a snack of apple wedges and peanut butter. With Sam happily occupied, she checked on Pete, who was back in bed.

"How's she doing?" Pete asked, eager for more news. But Anne didn't know any more than he did.

"I ought to go to the hospital," he said. "It's my fault, you know."

"It's no one's fault," Anne said firmly. My, but the Hardison family was big on blame. "Accidents happen. I'll stay here with Sam if you'd like to go to the hospital."

He coughed, long and hard. "I guess I'm not really up to it," he said when he caught his breath. "Don't ever get old, Anne."

"I don't like the alternative," she quipped. "Anyway, you're not old, you're just sick. Next week you'll be back to your usual frisky self."

"Hope so."

She tried to tuck in his blanket, but he waved her away. "Stop fussing. You gonna tell me that 'long story' now?"

She was really tired of justifying herself. ''I'm seeing Wade. We didn't want to tell anyone because it was all very new and fragile. But now everybody knows, and everybody's taking potshots at us. If you want to tell me what an idiot I am, you can stand in line.''

Pete surprised her by chuckling. ''Matters of the heart turn all of us into idiots at one time or another. But I always thought if you took a shine to any of my grandsons, it'd be Jeff.''

''Jeff's a fine person. But so is Wade. If you all would just give him half a chance—''

''Hold on there, girlie. It's not me giving him a hard time. Well, not that hard. I may needle him a bit, but I got a lot of respect for the boy, standing up to us like he did, then going out and making something of himself. Jonathan's the one who won't unbend. Judging from the talk I heard out of his mouth a while ago, that's not gonna change anytime soon. And with the way Jeff feels about you, he isn't likely to help.''

Anne was afraid Pete was right.

After dosing Pete with her own home remedy for coughing, which did not involve alcohol, Anne tackled another task she'd been dreading—calling her parents. It was ridiculous that at age twenty-five she was so worried about her parents' reactions to the choices she made, but the fact remained that she hated to disappoint them in any way. They had done so much to support her, in material as well as intangible ways.

She dialed the number. ''Hi, Mom.''

''Anne? Good heavens, where in the world are you? Is anything wrong?''

"As a matter of fact, yes. Kristin Hardison bumped her head and had to be taken to the hospital. I volunteered to take care of Sam and Pete—he's in bed with a cold." She didn't want to make the situation sound any more urgent than that, or her parents might drive to the hospital in Tyler themselves. She didn't figure the Hardisons needed outsiders descending on them right now; it was bad enough Anne herself had intruded.

"Is she all right?" Deborah asked breathlessly.

Anne sighed. "It was a pretty serious injury."

Deborah took a moment to absorb the news. "How did you end up with the Hardisons?"

Anne thought about how to answer that. But before she could formulate the correct response, Deborah gasped in her ear.

"It's Jeff, isn't it. Your mystery date. I noticed you two dancing at Pete's birthday party, and I wondered— Oh, I always thought you two would be so good together. I know now's not the ideal time for you to be hooking up with—"

"Mom, it's not—"

"—but he's such a *nice* young man. And I know I shouldn't be happy when you've just told me this terrible thing about little Kristin, but I can't help it."

"Mom, please, could I—"

But Deborah didn't hear Anne's objection. "Of course I'm still not pleased that you've jumped the gun, but you *have* known him forever, and I trust there'll be a wedding at some point—"

"Mother!"

"I have to go tell your father. Oh, and we should

send some flowers for Kristin, or a basket or something. Is she at Mother Frances?"

"Yes, but—"

"Fine, I'll take care of it. Don't worry, you just take care of Sam and Pete. Show the Hardisons what a responsible woman you've grown into." With that Deborah hung up.

Anne put her hand to her head, fighting off the ache there. Deborah was like a runaway freight train when she got an idea in her head. She would have Anne and Jeff married off in no time if Anne didn't do something.

But what?

WADE AND HIS TWO BROTHERS sat in an uneasy ceasefire, waiting for Kristin to come out of surgery. Their father joined them, but they were the only ones in the waiting room.

What was wrong with this picture? Wade asked himself. The answer was obvious. There were no women present. The Hardison men had a talent for disastrous relationships, or no relationships at all. Even Pete had managed to stave off Sally Enderlin, who was obviously besotted with him.

Wade didn't want to follow in the family tradition, but he sorely feared Jeff was right. He wasn't the right man for a woman like Anne, no matter how much he cared about her. Their relationship had a self-destruct mechanism installed. How could a big-city lawyer and a roaming rodeo cowboy possibly carry on a workable romance?

He had to do something. The picture before him—all those lonely men—positively terrified him. For

Sam's sake, if nothing else, he had to figure out a way to make things work with Anne, so someone in the family could set a decent example. But how?

A doctor in blue scrubs, his mask pulled down under his chin, entered the waiting room. Everyone sat up straighter, bracing themselves for the news. Jonathan sprang out of his chair, a bundle of nervous energy.

"Kristin came through the surgery just fine," the doctor said, and an audible sigh of relief rose in the room. "We'll know more when the anesthetic wears off, but at this point I'm cautiously optimistic."

"Can I see her?" Jonathan asked anxiously.

The doctor hesitated, then caved in. "For a minute or two. They're transferring her to intensive care. I'll send someone to get you when she's settled." He turned and left.

Jeff and their father couldn't get to Jonathan fast enough. They both hugged him, despite the fact they weren't a touchy-feely kind of family. Wade just sat there, knowing any gesture of support or affection would be spurned.

"What do you think, Dad?" Jonathan asked. "You think she'll be all right?"

"I'm not psychic," Edward Hardison said. "But I've seen plenty of patients fully recover after head injuries like Kristin's. We just have to wait and see. But she's crossed the first hurdle."

"She's a fighter," Jeff added.

Wade had nothing to add to that, so he said, "I'll go call Pete and let him know." He started to get up, but Jeff whipped out his cell phone.

"I'll do it," Jeff said.

So, they weren't going to let him participate in this small victory at all.

Well, he'd had it. He thought crises were supposed to bring families closer together, not drive them further apart. But apparently the Hardison family did everything wrong.

He stood suddenly and left. He'd banged his head against this brick wall enough times. If his birth family wasn't going to support him in the life he'd chosen or the woman he wanted to be with, if they were going to hold on to grudges and invent new reasons to despise him, then who needed them? He had another family, his rodeo buddies. They didn't kick a man when he was down.

He was surprised to see the weather had turned decidedly nastier while he'd been in the hospital. The temperature had dropped, and a fine mist was falling.

And he didn't have transportation.

Well, it wouldn't be the first time he'd thumbed his way someplace. He would hitch a ride back to the ranch, collect his horse and get the hell out of Dodge. He could rejoin the rodeo circuit, maybe do some saddle-bronc riding or earn a few extra bucks shoveling manure. He could still cheer on his friends.

And leave Anne?

Damn it. All right, he'd rent a stall somewhere for Traveler and stay in a motel. He'd stick around town until she accepted a job somewhere and left—or until she told him it was useless and to get lost. It might be time to give up on his family, but not on Anne, not after she'd gone public with their relationship.

He hiked to the main road and started walking, sticking his thumb out at each passing car.

It took about twenty minutes, by which time he was soaked through, but a kid in a tiny, beat-up truck picked him up and got him as far as the highway that would take him to Cottonwood. Another ten minutes and an eighteen-wheeler stopped. Wade got lucky—the guy was going all the way to Cottonwood on his way to points east.

"What's your story, cowboy?" the driver asked good-naturedly.

Wade supposed that was the price of his ride. "My family hates me, my horse is lame, my girl's about to move to New York or some damn place, *her* family hates me, and I don't know what to do with the rest of my life."

"Damn. I suppose you're broke, too."

Wade shook his head. "No, I'm not broke. Got a quarter-million dollars in the bank."

The driver thought he was kidding. He grinned. "With that kind of cash, seems you ought to be able to do whatever the hell you want with your life—including get the girl."

Though the words were thrown out casually, they made Wade think. His future was up to him. He'd always been one to go after what he wanted. He just had to figure out a plan.

It took Wade another thirty minutes to get from the highway, where the trucker dropped him off, to the ranch. He would have gone straight to the barn to pack up Traveler's gear first, because he wasn't up to facing anybody, including Pete and Sam. But he saw Anne's Mustang parked by the old barn. What was she doing here?

Drawn like a sailor to a siren's song, he went to

the house, noticing his father's SUV in the driveway. His dad had beat him back. But before he could make it to the front door, Anne came out. He stood aside, listening to his father thank her for her help, listening to the low murmur of her voice as she expressed some comforting words. Then the door closed, and she opened an umbrella and turned, intending to trudge down to the old barn and her car, he imagined.

She stopped, startled to see him. "You're soaking wet."

"That's what happens when you stand out in the rain." He wasn't about to tell her he'd been hitchhiking. It would only add to his irresponsible reputation. "Can you come to the barn with me for a few minutes?" The seductive scene he'd fantasized about earlier in the day—was it really today?—was only a distant memory at this point. He couldn't make love to Anne. But he did want to explain his intentions.

She checked her watch. "I really have to go."

"I know. We've kept you from your studying enough. Anne, I'm moving out."

Her face fell, reflecting disappointment. "Where are you going?"

He shrugged. "Where I don't have to face Jonathan every day. I could take him being wary of me, but I can't handle him hating me."

"Wade, he doesn't hate you. He's in the middle of a crisis. Give him a chance to calm down."

"I want to do that—I know it's what I *should* do—but I can't make myself." It just hurt too damn much.

"Why don't you talk to your father? Maybe you can stay with him."

Wade shook his head. "He's not any better."

"Just try. If you walk out now, it's as good as admitting Jonathan is right about you. The things he said aren't true. They're not right, and you need to set him straight."

"Maybe that's how you handle conflicts in your family, but the Hardisons are different. I wouldn't know how to begin to straighten this out."

"Running isn't the answer. Last time you ran, you stayed gone thirteen years."

He couldn't meet her earnest gaze. She had no idea what she was asking of him. "I'll call you when I've settled somewhere."

He couldn't interpret the look she gave him. Maybe she pitied him, or maybe she just didn't want him to call. If she was worried about what her parents would think, it would only get worse, now that no one was speaking to him.

He turned and walked toward the new barn, while he still had the courage to go against her wishes.

WHEN ANNE GOT HOME, her mother was waiting for her. "I just spoke to Edward Hardison," she said without preamble the moment Anne walked through the door.

Anne cringed. "Then I suppose he, um, filled you in."

"Oh, yes. When I mentioned how pleased I was that you and Jeff were seeing each other socially, he was quite perplexed. He was under the impression it was you and his youngest son who were...romantically involved."

Anne said nothing. What was there to say at this point?

"I'd like to hear the truth from my own daughter. For a change."

"I didn't lie to you," Anne said hotly. "You assumed it was Jeff, and then you were off as if a team of wild horses was dragging you. I tried to interrupt, but you weren't listening. You wouldn't listen to anything, anyway, except what you wanted to hear."

Anne hung her denim jacket on a hook by the garage door. She longed to flee to her room, but it was time to deal with her mother, adult-to-adult—not act like a teenager.

When she looked at Deborah again, her mother's face had paled. "Is that what you really think?"

"You have this image of me, the perfect daughter. And you don't want to hear about anything that conflicts with that image. Well, I'm not perfect. I make mistakes, lots of them, as I so adequately proved last summer."

"And I don't think I was overly harsh or judgmental about that, was I?"

Anne softened. "No. You were loving and supportive. I couldn't have wished for a better mother. But since then, it's like you and Dad are more determined than ever to get me back on track and keep me there. And I'm realizing more and more that this track I've been on...well, it might not be quite right for me."

"Is that what getting pregnant was all about? Forcing a change in plans?"

Anne sat down at the breakfast bar. "I don't know. Maybe. I didn't do it on purpose, but I can't deny part of me was relieved to postpone my career plans."

"Anne, for heaven's sake, if you don't want to be a lawyer, then just be something else. Don't go out and make crazy decisions that will force alternative plans into your life."

"You think my seeing Wade is crazy?"

"Frankly, yes. I don't see how you could be even slightly compatible."

"We are, though."

"Oh, Anne. When your father finds out, he'll hit the roof."

"Then he'll just have to hit the roof. You know I love both of you, and I hate causing you to be upset and worried. I didn't plan this thing with Wade. It just happened. And you don't have to worry about it derailing my career plans. I'm still planning to be a lawyer."

"But how can you and Wade…I mean…"

"There *is* no me and Wade. He's moving on. So you can stop worrying." She tried to sound dismissive, like it didn't matter to her. But the idea of Wade leaving Cottonwood, forever this time, was like a drill straight into the core of her heart.

ANNE DIDN'T HEAR from Wade that day or the day after. But she did hear from Jeff, who politely requested that she drop by his office. She assumed it had something to do with her blood tests. She certainly hoped he wasn't going to interrogate her further about Wade. She'd had quite enough of that.

Molly ushered Anne into Jeff's office, where she was left to fidget for a few minutes. When Jeff finally appeared, his expression was somber.

Anne shivered, not because she was cold, but because she suddenly dreaded the conversation to come.

If her blood tests had come out normal, he never would have called her in for this special conference.

Sitting across from her, his white coat absent, he seemed unusually human to her. He had shed his normal doctorly detachment, she realized, and was looking at her now not as a doctor to a patient, and not as a potential lover, but as a friend. She liked him much better this way.

"How's Kristin doing?" she asked, though her parents had been in touch with Edward and had kept Anne informed.

Jeff smiled slightly. "She's doing great. Real cranky about being confined to a hospital bed, and that's a good sign."

"Did she tell you what happened?"

"Near as we can figure, she woke up from her nap feeling better, and decided to turn her bed into a trampoline."

Exactly as Anne had guessed. "I hope Jonathan isn't still blaming Wade."

Jeff shrugged, looking uneasy. "Doesn't matter. Wade's not there to blame anymore."

Anne felt a vacuum in her chest. "Where is he?" she asked, trying not to sound as anxious as she felt. He'd warned her he was leaving, but she'd been praying he would change his mind.

"You don't know? I was kind of hoping you would."

"He hasn't contacted me." And no amount of staring at the phone had changed that.

"He packed up and took off without a word that evening, after Kristin's surgery. I was hoping you might know where he'd gone."

She shook her head. "But if I did know, what would you do? Try to drag him back to the ranch so you can heap more abuse on him? I mean, really, Jeff, do you blame him for leaving?"

A look of shame washed over Jeff's face. "No. That's why I want to find him. To apologize. I thought about what you said at the hospital, and I decided you're right. We haven't given Wade a chance. We haven't even tried to find out what kind of person he grew up to be. We just keep harping on the same old sins that we've built up in our minds. I talked to Dad and Granddad, and they agree with me."

"What about Jonathan?"

Jeff shook his head. "Wade's not the only hard-headed one in the bunch. I can't speak for Jon, but Wade won't get through to him if he doesn't stick around."

"I'm sure he'll surface, when everyone's had a chance to cool off," Anne said, hoping against hope she spoke the truth. She'd known all along her relationship with Wade, if you could call it that, was doomed. She'd entertained any number of uncomfortable fantasies that featured tearful goodbye scenes, but she'd never imagined that he would just disappear from her life without a word—the way she once had from his. But maybe that was poetic justice.

"If I talk to him first, I'll let him know what you just told me," Anne said. "Right now he feels like the whole family, and possibly the whole world, is against him."

"Even you?"

"Maybe especially me. I argued with him the night he left."

"He's not that easy to get along with."

"You're doing it again. I've found him exceptionally easy to get along with." Boy, was that an understatement. "Most of the time, anyway."

Jeff nodded and smiled, embarrassed. "Okay, I'll work on the attitude. Is there anything you want to talk about? I mean, with you and Wade?"

"You mean, medically?" Anne hoped he was kidding.

"You're protecting yourself?"

"I don't want to talk about me and Wade. That's not why you asked me here."

"No."

"So, spill it," she said, mentally bracing herself. "What's wrong with me?"

He didn't beat around the bush. "Just what I suspected. You carry the gene for a heart defect."

Anne felt like someone had splashed ice water in her face. *She had a genetic defect.*

"Although we can't be sure," Jeff continued in his even, measured tones, "that's probably why you miscarried. Miscarriages usually occur because something is wrong with the developing embryo. It's nature's not-so-kind way of housekeeping."

Anne took a deep breath, trying to sort out the implications. "So is that why my mother lost all those babies?"

"Your family history of miscarriages is one of the reasons I suspected a genetic component. Again, we can't know for sure, but in all likelihood both of your parents carry the gene."

"But Mom had me with no problems. You said yourself, my heart is terrific."

"It has to do with how the chromosomes from mother and father combine. For a defect to manifest, both parents have to carry the gene, and they both have to give it to the offspring. If the baby receives only one, she develops normally, but she's a carrier."

"Me." Anne asked the question she'd been avoiding. "Does that mean I can never have children?"

"No, not at all. You'll have problems only if the father carries the same defective gene."

"But, just for discussion's sake, I can't have children with certain, particular men who have the gene."

"You could. But I wouldn't recommend it. You might have a series of miscarriages, like your mother. And even if you carried a full-term child, it might exhibit the birth defect."

Anne shuddered. "That would be terrible. I don't know how my mother survived losing so many babies." Losing one was bad enough. "Is this bad-heart gene very common?" Just ask the right questions. *Pretend you're researching for a case.*

"More common than people think. Maybe six or seven percent of the population is affected." Jeff trod carefully with his next question. "As I understand it, though, the father of your child is out of the picture, right?"

"Um, yes." She hated lying, but she couldn't risk Wade's family knowing he'd fathered a child out of wedlock. That would just be more evidence of Wade's lack of character—and possibly the nail in the coffin of the Hardison reconciliation.

"Then there's nothing to worry about. You'll need

to take precautions before getting pregnant in the future. The potential father would need to be tested to be sure he doesn't carry the same gene, but the chances of that are relatively small.''

''Okay, I understand.'' Only too well.

''Are you still on speaking terms with the father?'' Jeff asked matter-of-factly.

Anne couldn't answer. Her throat felt like it was closing up.

''Maybe that's none of my business. But if you talk to him, you might let him know the circumstances. Whoever he is, he should have a blood test before he fathers any more children. I'm sure you'll agree it's better to prevent a doomed pregnancy before it happens.''

Anne just nodded numbly and tried to stop shaking. Of course, she wouldn't want any other woman to go through losing a baby if she didn't have to. She looked everywhere but at Jeff.

''Anne, please, don't take this so hard. It's not your fault. You can definitely have more children.''

She nodded again, swallowed, and with a concerted effort got hold of her feelings. This wasn't the end of the world. ''I know. I just feel scared, knowing I have some rogue killer gene roaming around my body.''

''*Everyone* has a few rotten genes. Even in my family.''

Anne sat up a little straighter. ''Really?'' Her head swam with the implications. If Wade carried the gene, his brothers might, too. And Sam and Kristin.

''We all have flat feet.''

''Oh. Have you ever, you know, out of curiosity, had your own blood tested?''

"Who, me? No way. I'll let you in on a little secret." He looked left, then right, with exaggerated paranoia, then whispered, "I'm afraid of needles, too."

Anne managed to smile, appreciating Jeff's attempt to cheer her up, but her smile faded the minute she cleared his office. Much as she hated to admit it, she had a moral obligation to inform Wade about his genetic problem. Which meant she couldn't fudge and waffle anymore. She had to tell him about the pregnancy.

But how could she do that if she couldn't find him?

Chapter Ten

The night Wade left the ranch, he drove his truck and trailer around the outskirts of Cottonwood, trying to recall where he'd seen a sign: Horses Boarded. Finally he remembered. It was the day he and Anne had gone on the picnic. Sally Enderlin's place, which butted up against Hardison land. It was maybe a little too close to the ranch for comfort, but chances were no one would even realize he was there, or care.

Sally would be a tonic to his soul. She understood a lot about his family, and she would take him in without questions. And she wouldn't talk—not even to Pete.

"Of course, I'll pay you rent," Wade said as Sally showed him her barn.

"Oh, don't be silly," she said. "You're like family, like my own grandson. I'm happy to give you a safe place to roost while you sort things out with your brother. In fact, you want me to go over there right now and talk some sense into him?"

Wade smiled at the picture of wiry Sally, sitting Jonathan down like a naughty first grader and lecturing to him. "Nah, this'll work itself out," he said with more optimism than he felt.

Sally helped him unload Traveler and his gear. Fortunately the horse was so used to traveling that the stress of the move didn't bother him at all. He checked out his new pasture and a couple of fat old mares he shared it with, then settled down to graze. He was walking better, Wade had noted with some relief. The limp was far less pronounced.

Sally offered Wade the use of her foreman's house, where he could have some privacy. Currently it was vacant. She didn't have much left of her farm, she admitted, and she'd had to let her one employee go. Wade offered to do some chores for her in exchange for her hospitality.

"I already planned on getting some work out of you," she said with a chuckle. "A strapping young man like you can't sit around idle."

The next day she worked him like an ox, for which he was grateful. Working his body hard kept him from having to think. But on the following day, he realized he was wasting good time. Who knew how many days he had left with Anne?

So that morning, after he helped Sally water and feed her animals, he showered, put on his best shirt and his least-faded jeans and drove to Anne's parents' house.

Deborah Chatsworth answered the door. She was an incredibly well-put-together woman, dressed as if she were on her way to church. He knew Anne's parents were older, well into their sixties, but neither of them looked it.

Deborah frowned. "I assume you're here to see Anne."

He didn't know how much Anne's mother knew of his relationship with her daughter, but he decided to keep things simple.

"Yes, ma'am. Is she home?"

"I'll see." She left him standing on the front porch. Didn't even ask him in. This didn't bode well. That "I'll see" meant she would check with Anne and find out whether her daughter would consent to see him.

If she didn't, what would he do? Storm the house? Wait until nighttime and climb a tree up to Anne's window? Maybe he should have called first, but he'd been worried Anne would tell him not to come. If she was going to call it quits, he wanted her to do it in person.

A few minutes later the front door opened again, revealing Anne's mother looking even more disapproving than before. Her lips were pressed together in a thin line, her brow deeply furrowed.

"She'll be down in a minute. Please don't keep her long. She has a lot of work to do."

Wade resisted the urge to salute and say, Yes, ma'am. Apparently Anne hadn't inherited her steel backbone solely from her father.

Anne herself appeared a minute or two later dressed in forest-green sweatpants and a matching shirt that hung almost to her knees. She was obviously dressed for comfort, not for style, which only made sense since she was studying and working on her job search. But he missed his Annie.

She didn't greet him with a welcoming smile. Instead she looked surprised and anxious. "Wade, where have you been?"

He didn't want to have this conversation with her on her parents' front porch. So instead of answering, he asked, "Do you want to visit Kristin? I'm heading out that way, and I could use the company."

She obviously hadn't expected that question.

"You could bring your books along," he continued. "You can drive, and I'll ask you questions out of that bar review book."

Finally she smiled. "That's not necessary. Give me five minutes to change my clothes." She opened the front door wider and allowed him inside, but just to the entry hall. He waited there for her while she changed, unable to stop himself from imagining her peeling off those shapeless sweats and revealing her sweet, sexy body.

While he waited, Deborah passed by with a watering can, on her way to tend some plants in the living room's bay window. She did a double take, as if to say, You're still here? Then she nodded, walked on, stopped, turned back.

"I will personally kick you to Cleveland if you do anything to hurt my daughter. She's been through a lot. She doesn't need any extra stress."

Lord, the woman was downright scary. "Ma'am, I have no intention of doing anything to hurt Anne. I have nothing but the greatest respect for her."

"You think disappearing for two days without a word shows respect?"

She had him there. "No, it doesn't. Anne was angry at me, and I thought we both needed to cool off. It didn't occur to me she would be worried."

"Maybe among your rodeo friends people come and go and no one worries, but around here it's just not done."

"I'll apologize."

Deborah's expression said, That's not enough. But she left to tend to her plants rather than pursue the matter. As he waited for Anne, he could hear her rustling around in the living room, a praying mantis ready to pounce on an unsuspecting insect at the least movement.

Anne came downstairs a few moments later, looking like a real heartbreaker in jeans and a figure-revealing sweater. She'd done something to her hair, too. It was still pulled back, but it looked softer somehow. She grabbed a leather jacket and purse from the coat tree in the entry hall, called a vague goodbye to her mother, and headed out the front door.

She said nothing until they were in the car. Finally he spoke first.

"I told your mother I would apologize for disappearing. I didn't realize anyone would worry."

"Of course you did. You ran off for the precise reason that you knew everyone would wonder and worry about you. It's your revenge."

"Ouch."

"Just calling it like I see it."

"You might be wrong, Lawyer Anne. I needed to remove myself from the ranch before someone threw a punch. Probably me, since I'm the one with the hot head, or so everyone says. They might even be right about that."

"You could have let someone know where you were."

"You're right. I'm not used to accounting for my whereabouts, and I just wasn't thinking. I really am sorry."

She relaxed a bit after that. "Apology accepted. Have you talked to Jeff? Or your father?"

"No. I'll call one of them and let 'em know where I am."

"Good. And you might be surprised at what happens."

"What do you mean?"

"Jeff wants to do a little apologizing of his own, and so do your father and grandfather. They realized they haven't given you a fair chance."

Wade *was* surprised to hear that. Surprised and amazingly gratified. He'd tried to tell himself, the last couple of days, that he didn't care what they thought of him. But of course he cared. "What about Jonathan?"

Anne shrugged. "No word from him. Will he be okay with your visiting Kristin?"

"Probably not. I'm hoping I won't run into him. But I have to see her. I want to see for myself she's doing okay."

"You're really crazy about her, aren't you?"

"Yeah. Both of those kids are great, amazing. I always liked kids, but I never was close to any till Sam and Kristin. They're so...so innocent. So accepting. God knows what they've heard about their uncle Wade, but they don't care. They judge me by what they see here and now."

Anne put her hand on his arm. "There's something I should tell you."

Hell. He pulled over to the shoulder and stopped.

"What are you doing?" She sounded alarmed.

"I can't stand it anymore. I have to kiss you."

Her eyes widened, but she didn't resist when he unhooked his seat belt and slid over next to her, then put his arms around her and brought his mouth down on hers, none too gently. It had been too long.

She came alive in his arms, the passionate, no-holds-barred Annie he adored. "You're wearing perfume," he whispered into her ear just before he tickled it with his tongue.

"You don't like it?" she asked, her voice raspy.

"No, I love it."

"It's just a sample from a drugstore."

"I'll buy you a gallon of it. It turns me on."

"Seems you don't need any help in that department."

He found her mouth again, this time exploring with his tongue. He silently cursed the fact they didn't have any real privacy. If they did, he would make love to her the way it was meant to be done—in a soft bed with clean sheets.

"Wade..."

"I know, I know." He forced himself to back away, giving her nose a quick peck as he retreated. "I could take you to my new digs, but it's pretty humble."

"You're worried about that? After making love to me in a horse trailer?"

"Are you saying yes?"

She ducked her head and looked out the window. "I'm saying I'd like to see where you've been staying, after we visit Kristin."

His own personal gloom lifted. Everything would

look better once he had Anne in his arms and in his bed—and he was pretty confident that was where she'd end up. But first, the hospital.

AS ANNE RODE in Wade's truck on the way to the hospital in Tyler, she kept thinking how relieved she was to see him again. She'd been terribly afraid he'd left, for good this time. Thank goodness he hadn't made that decision—not just for herself, but for his relationship with his family. Going through life angry at your own flesh and blood was no way to live. She really believed that if Wade wanted to be happy, he had to resolve the problems with Jonathan.

On the other hand, if he'd disappeared, she'd have been spared the trauma of telling him about the miscarriage and the bad gene. She'd almost found the courage just now. But then he'd kissed her and her mind had gone blank.

"How's Traveler?" she asked.

"A lot better. The swelling's gone down and he's hardly favoring the leg at all now. Doc Chandler said he might be ready for Kansas City after all."

"That's great!" And not so great. The American Royal Rodeo in Kansas City was only two weeks away. Of course, her own time in Cottonwood was growing short, too. She had several fantastic job offers on the table, and her father was urging her to make a decision.

"I think it has to do with the other horses he's stabled with," Wade continued. "Flashy Cimmaron, with her mile-long pedigree, didn't interest him in the least, but these two fat old mares, who do nothing but stand around and munch grass, threw him into a tizzy. He's been trying to impress them.''

''Nothing like a little romance to perk you up,'' Anne said, knowing she'd never spoken truer words. Her relationship with Wade had changed her whole outlook on life. Suddenly there were things more important than test scores and GPA and job interviews. For years she'd postponed living her life, thinking that was something she would have time for later. But one never knew how much time was left. Kristin's accident had brought that fact home.

So why hadn't she done anything about it? She was still planning to accept a job with a huge firm in a huge city. A young law associate's back-breaking workload was an investment in the future, she knew. By putting in her time, she could have anything she wanted later in life—early retirement, travel, luxuries. But the price for that security was steep. She'd never before questioned her commitment, her willingness to pay the price. Now she did.

When Anne and Wade got to the hospital, they had to hunt around for Kristin because she'd been moved out of intensive care to a children's ward with about a dozen other kids. When Wade finally spotted her, he grinned like a little boy who'd just been presented with an ice-cream sundae.

Kristin sat cross-legged in her bed, working industriously on a coloring book. Her head was swathed in bandages and she had an IV in her arm, but otherwise she appeared pretty healthy. She looked up when Wade headed her way, almost as if she had radar for him.

Her face lit up. ''Uncle Wade!''

But Kristin wasn't alone. Jonathan sat by her bed, and the expression on his face could have derailed a train. Anne was glad she'd come. She wasn't going to let Jonathan diminish Wade in Kristin's eyes, no matter how determined he was that Wade was the enemy.

"Hey, doodlebug!" Wade said. But he stopped before he reached the bed and formally addressed his brother. "Jonathan, do I have your permission to visit with Kristin for a few minutes?"

It was the right approach, Anne realized. Kristin, obviously picking up on the tension, looked anxiously at her father for the answer to Wade's question. Jonathan might still harbor a powerful grudge against Wade, but he wasn't going to do anything to upset or disappoint Kristin.

Jonathan spared Anne a look, silently accusing her of consorting with the enemy, then gave a curt nod. "I'm going to get a bite to eat. It'll take about thirty minutes." He paused and looked at his watch. "Be gone when I get back."

Anne sent Jonathan a pleading look, but he paid no attention to her. He gave Kristin a quick kiss on the cheek before departing, but Kristin's eyes were on Wade, whom she clearly adored.

Wade pulled the chair out for Anne but remained standing himself. "So, what happened to you?" Wade asked Kristin in a teasing voice.

"The doctor, um, did an op'ration on my head. They had to cut my hair off and everything."

"They sure did. I don't know, Anne, what do you think? Will Kristin start a new fashion trend?"

Half of Kristin's head had been shaved, while the

other half was braided and hung down to her shoulder. Anne smiled. ‘‘Pretty stylish. Maybe I should do my hair like that.’’

Kristin laughed. She didn't appear to be in much discomfort, though she looked pale.

Wade reached into the shopping bag he'd brought with him and pulled out a horse puppet. It was tan with a black mane. He stuck it on his hand. ‘‘Hi, Kristin,’’ he said in a pseudo Mr. Ed voice. ‘‘You haven't been to the barn lately to see me.’’

Kristin caught on right away, directly addressing the puppet. ‘‘Traveler! I can't go to the barn 'cause I hurt my head.’’

‘‘And I hurt my leg. We're twins,’’ Traveler the puppet said.

‘‘We're not twins. You're a horse,’’ Kristin retorted, offended at the very idea.

And that was how it went for several minutes. Wade gently teased, Kristin laughed. She showed him her coloring book, in which she'd colored everything purple because grape was her favorite crayon. She talked about the cartoon characters decorating her hospital gown, which Wade greatly admired. He asked her if she'd watched *Fairy Princess,* which was her favorite TV program, and she excitedly recounted the whole plot.

He was so good with kids. He really deserved to have a herd of his own. Anne supposed it was a good thing she and Wade were doomed to separate, because she would never be able to give him children.

That realization, so unexpected, brought tears to her eyes. She'd never really thought much about having children, not until her pregnancy. She'd wanted that baby with a fierce maternal instinct that had surprised her and everyone around her. After the miscarriage she'd tried to convince herself she didn't really want kids, at least not for years and years. Her strategy was to ruthlessly squelch any thoughts of babies or children. It hadn't worked that well at the time.

Now suddenly that strategy didn't work at all. She wanted children, sooner rather than later. She wanted Wade's children, children she could never have. Of all the ridiculous conclusions to reach…

She had to get out of there before Wade noticed her crying. She stood abruptly. "Back in a minute," she managed before dashing to the exit of the children's ward.

She found a bathroom, sobbed a few times, then pressed a wet paper towel to her face and the back of her neck until she brought herself under control. After a quick makeup repair and quite a few deep breaths, she felt ready to face Wade again, barely.

He was pacing the hallway outside the ladies' room when she emerged. He looked up anxiously. "Anne? Are you okay?"

"I'm fine." She looked everywhere but in his eyes.

"You were crying."

"Oh, that." She waved away his concern. "It just suddenly struck me how close we came to losing Kristin, that's all."

Wade didn't look like he believed her, but he didn't press.

"Your visit must have done Kristin a world of good."

"I bet Jonathan doesn't think that."

"Hey, at least he let you visit. That's progress."

Wade slung a casual arm around Anne's shoulders as they headed for the elevator. "Progress measured in inches, but I'll take it."

Anne liked having Wade's arm around her, more than she cared to admit. She relished the envious looks she got from several nurses, who probably wondered how an ordinary-looking woman such as herself had managed to land such a handsome, sexy cowboy.

"Do you really want to see my new place?" Wade asked casually once they were inside his truck. "It's not much, but it has a few things to recommend it."

"Like what?"

He tossed her a wicked grin. "A queen-size bed, for starters."

She answered his grin with one of her own. No mistaking Wade's intentions this time. He wanted to make love to her. The cautious law student in her, the one who was Deborah Chatsworth's daughter, warned her to use her brain for once where Wade was concerned and request that he take her straight home.

Unfortunately, her alter-ego, Annie, was far stronger at the moment than good-girl Anne. This was probably her last chance to enjoy lovemaking with Wade, because after she told him about the baby, he probably wouldn't speak to her, much less share his body with her. She wasn't going to pass up the opportunity, selfish wretch that she was. She'd been using this excuse for a while—but this was the last time, really.

Wade pulled the truck into the driveway of Sally Enderlin's place.

"You mean you've been staying here? Right next door the whole time?"

"Mmm-hmm." He drove all the way around to the back of the house. Two hundred feet farther down the drive stood a cottage, a miniature version of the main house. It looked as if someone had made recent repairs to the porch and trimmed the trees and bushes around it. "I bunk here, in the foreman's cottage."

"How charming," Anne couldn't help saying. She liked old houses, probably because she'd never lived in one.

"*Rustic* might be a better description. I finally got the shower to work, but there's no hot water, and the kitchen hasn't been updated since the Dark Ages."

"Well, you're not planning to live here long, right?"

He cut the engine, then gave her his full attention. "I'm not going back to the ranch unless Jonathan asks me." They got out of the truck.

"I realize that," she said as they mounted the porch steps. "I don't blame you. I just wondered when you'll be rejoining the rodeo circuit."

"Not till the Royal. That starts in two weeks." He didn't sound too thrilled about it. He let her inside the cottage, then closed only the screen door to bring in some fresh air, which the cottage sorely needed. "How's your job search shaping up?"

"I have offers from two of my A-list firms. I'll be making a decision soon." She realized she sounded no more thrilled with her plans than he did.

"What firms?" he wanted to know.

"One's in Boston. One's in Miami." She tried to muster some enthusiasm. "It's strange to think I'll be moving to one of those cities. I've never lived outside Texas.'' She knew she should sit down. But now that she was here, she felt antsy. She'd been itching to get her hands on Wade all day—for several days, actually—and finally they had some privacy. She just didn't know where to begin.

''Aren't any of your A-list law firms in Dallas?'' Wade asked.

She shook her head. ''Only one, and when I interviewed there, I hated the place.''

''You'll come back to visit your folks, though.''

''Maybe once or twice a year. You know, you could always come visit me,'' she said offhandedly.

''Not many rodeos in Boston.''

''Take a vacation, then.''

He sighed. ''You don't really think an occasional visit would be enough, do you?''

She gave up on making a quick segue to the bedroom and settled for slumping into a nearby, nubby brown chair. ''No.'' She couldn't see Wade maintaining a relationship with a woman hundreds of miles away. Phone calls and letters just wouldn't do it. On the circuit he was constantly barraged by hungry, attractive females, and he would succumb to temptation sooner or later. She would worry about that constantly. She got insanely jealous just wondering what women he'd been with over the summer, while she'd been pregnant with his child.

''Life is for living, Anne. Let's not waste the whole damn day worrying about what we can't have. We've got each other right now, and sometimes living for the moment isn't such a bad idea.''

He held out his hand, and she took it. He was so

right. She'd spent her whole life planning and preparing. The only time she'd really, really lived was that wild weekend when she became Annie.

He pulled her to her feet, and she went straight into his arms. They kissed, wrapped around each other, pressing their bodies as close as they could get. She absorbed every sensation—the sandpaper texture of his cheek and chin on her face, the smell of soap and starch on his collar, the silkiness of his thick, dark hair, the hard muscles of his chest against her breasts.

He moved his hand to her bottom, pressing her hips against his arousal. The passion she'd obviously awakened in him was a tremendous turn-on. She reveled in her feminine power over him even as she acknowledged her own weakness where he was concerned. He could ask her for almost anything, and she would do her best to give it.

And what if he asked you to give up law? What if he asked her to become a rodeo wife, traveling the country with him, cheering him on, living in his trailer with no possessions but the clothes on her back?

Oddly the possibility had its appealing qualities. But she knew that, in the long run, she had to do something with her brain. She couldn't live her life as some man's cheerleader and nothing for herself, even if the man was Wade.

Besides, he hadn't asked her.

Wade groaned, then scooped her into his arms. "I've got to get you naked, Annie."

She didn't even bristle at the use of her alter-ego name. He'd been right all along: Annie was part of her, a part she could no longer hide or deny. Annie was all sexy woman, and right now she was in control, having pushed almost-lawyer Anne far into the background. Anne couldn't have come up with the answer to the simplest question she might encounter on the bar exam.

She spared a quick glance around the bedroom, which was as spartan as the rest of the house. But the iron bed appeared to be made up with crisp, white cotton sheets, and a window had been left open, chasing out any lingering mustiness. An old chair and beat-up dresser completed the furnishings. The closet door was open, revealing two shirts hanging on the bar and one pair of boots.

He had so little and didn't seem to care. She wished she could be like that. She wished she could just not care about salaries and benefit packages and career tracks.

Wade laid her on the bed and made good his promise to get her naked. When he had her down to her underthings—another sexy little bra-and-panty set, pale blue this time, which she'd quickly donned when she'd changed her clothes—he pulled her to a sitting position and went to work on her hair, pulling out the pins and combs one by one until it fell loose in a fluffy red cloud.

She liked the feel of her hair on her bare shoulders. She gave her head a shake, smiling at Wade.

He didn't smile back. In fact, he looked unusually somber, and she wondered what he was thinking.

A cool breeze ruffled the organdy curtains, and Anne shivered.

"Cold?" Wade asked as he stripped off his own shirt. His body was so gorgeous—all smooth tanned skin over uncompromising muscle and sinew and bone—that for a moment she couldn't say anything.

"I'm sure you'll warm me up," she finally said.

He moved a little faster as he shucked the rest of his clothes. She found herself perversely wishing she wasn't protected by birth-control pills. Darn it, she wanted a baby, Wade's baby.

Then she shuddered at the thought of the consequences. She couldn't survive another miscarriage.

She might as well wish for the moon.

Chapter Eleven

Wade joined Anne on the bed, stretching her out on her back and lying atop her. He kissed her thoroughly while exploring her quivering body with warm, curious hands. The bra didn't last long, and her panties soon followed the bra. Wade spent what seemed like hours just kissing her breasts, testing their weight in his palms, teasing the nipples with his tongue until she ached all over.

The exciting thing was, she knew he'd hardly begun his sweet torture. He kissed her in places she never imagined being kissed, each new assault of lips and tongue drawing her further into the passionate haze he'd created.

He parted her legs and deftly probed the most sensitive area on her body, making her writhe with pleasure and excitement, but he knew just when to pull back, denying her the ultimate physical release.

"Wade. I want you inside me."

"I want that, too, angel. I just don't want to rush things."

"Trust me, you're not rushing."

He ran his hand from her hip all the way up her

body, eventually caressing her face. "How much do you want your big boy?"

"A lot."

"How much?"

"I'll beg."

He chuckled. "No begging."

"Then what's your price?"

"I'll decide later."

She spread her legs and welcomed him, gasping as he sought entrance. He took his time, filling her slowly, then gently rocking in a rhythm as timeless as the oceans. Like dancing, she thought, hearing a low, sexy saxophone in her head.

She was no longer chilled. In fact, as they accelerated their lovemaking, she got short of breath, and her skin grew moist with perspiration.

Toward the end he slid his arms under her and embraced her tenderly. He held her like that, like something precious, as he spilled his seed inside her. Seeds that could never take root. Never, not ever.

She'd thought it before, but she knew it for sure now. She was deeply, irrevocably in love with Wade Hardison. The realization brought equal amounts of joy and terror, and it all culminated in a beautiful climax that seemed to go on and on, bringing tears to her eyes.

"That's perfect, darlin'," he soothed. "You're incredible, just incredible."

"Wade?"

"Yes, darlin'?" He rolled to the side, taking some of his weight off her. Then he kissed her eyelids, no doubt tasting her tears. "I didn't hurt you, did I?"

"No. I know you're not supposed to say mushy things after making love—"

"Why not?"

"Because usually people don't mean what they say in bed. But I just have to say, no matter what happens, I…you're…you mean something to me." There, she'd just made a complete ass of herself. The only way it could have been worse was if she'd actually said, "I love you."

He hugged her close again. "You just made this a real good day for me." Then he pulled away and looked at her. "What do you mean, 'no matter what happens'?"

"Just that we're going to be separated. No two ways about it."

"We'll work it out," he soothed.

"But you just said—"

"I was trying to be cool by saying it wouldn't work. I didn't want you to think I was hopelessly sappy and naive."

"That was before you realized I'm sappy and naive."

He smoothed her hair away from her face. "That's what makes us so perfect for each other."

Perfect. Right. She'd never known two people who were less perfect for each other.

"I knew we were good together that first weekend. I was going to ask you to stay with me. That was before I knew you were law-firm bait."

"I had no idea. I thought I was just another conquest."

"I hope you know better now."

"I do." At least, she thought she did.

"So why did you get on the pill?" Wade asked out of the blue.

"Jeff prescribed them. To regulate my cycle after—"

Wade gave a snort of disgust. "Oh, that's rich. Wonder what he had in mind?"

"Wade, now just stop it. There were very good medical reasons at the time. Anyway, I thought reliable birth control was a sensible precaution—in case we ran into each other again."

"Just me?"

"Yes, just you. I don't sleep around."

"And what about Annie?"

"Annie's wild, but she's loyal."

He grinned sideways at her, and she decided that in her roundabout way she'd given him the answer he wanted. At least she'd derailed his suspicious thoughts about Jeff.

She'd also, once again, managed to sidestep a perfectly good opening to tell him about the miscarriage. She was a complete coward. But telling him while they were in bed didn't seem right.

The fact was, no time seemed right.

WADE DELAYED getting out of bed, even though he knew he ought to. He hated putting on clothes after making love to Anne, because he never knew when they'd be together again, if ever. Every time he was with her, the silken bonds between them grew tighter and he became less tolerant of the idea of living without her.

At least she'd admitted she had feelings for him. Maybe they weren't as deep as his, but she was moving in the right direction. Still, their time together was slipping away, just like the sun was slipping low on the horizon. He had to do something—and it had to be something dramatic, some grand gesture that would bind her to him.

He wanted to marry Anne someday, but right now he couldn't even mention it. Jonathan had been right when he'd said Wade had nothing to offer someone like Anne. But that wouldn't always be the case. If he won the big prize money in Kansas City, he'd have enough to make a start on that stud farm. Once he had the property and some breeding stock, he could hold his own. Sally supported herself with just a few goats, chickens, rabbits and some beehives. It couldn't be that hard.

At least he would be in one place to call home. Then he could start thinking about the rodeo camp—and making the woman in his life a permanent installation. Even Anne's parents would feel better about her settling down with a horse breeder than an itinerant calf roper.

He hadn't yet worked out how they would mesh her law career with his plans, but there had to be a way.

"Wade?"

He jumped, realizing he'd been staring up at the ceiling, spinning his dreams. He had a long row to hoe, and he had to take that first step—the one that would bring Anne solidly into his dream, a partner. But he was stuck on exactly what that step would be.

"You were a million miles away," she said. "What on earth were you thinking about?"

He couldn't tell her, not yet. He had to practice

what he would say. "I was thinking about my future."

"Kansas City?"

"For starters." Damn, did she think he didn't live beyond the next two weeks? He had to make her see there was more to him than that. "But I better get my head out of the clouds. I have hungry animals to take care of."

He and Anne dragged themselves out of bed, cleaned up, dressed.

Anne slid her feet into her loafers, then checked her appearance in the wavy dresser mirror. "Want some help with your chores?"

"I was hoping you'd ask. Not ready to face the books again?"

She frowned. "Not yet. My dad's already disappointed in me. Might as well live up to his expectations."

"How could anyone be disappointed in you? Top of your class, gonna get hired by a top law firm. And it's not like you'll flunk the bar. I mean, let's get real."

"There are all kinds of ways to disappoint."

"If the worst thing you ever do is carry on with a cowboy for a few weeks, your dad has nothing to worry about."

She smiled, but there was a shadow across her face. He'd seen it before, and he didn't know what it meant. He sensed a well of sadness in Anne sometimes. It made him want to hold her, shelter her, stop anything from ever hurting her again.

Anne helped him round up the horses, stable them, feed them—each with its own special diet—and fill the watering troughs. Goats, rabbits and chickens came next. Anne got a kick out of the bunnies. She picked a black Angora baby to carry around with her for a few minutes, threatening to slip it into her purse and take it home.

"Your mother would love it," Wade said. "It could live in her garden."

"Oh, right." Reluctantly Anne put the rabbit back in its hutch. "I suppose you'd better take me home."

"You can't just bring your books over here and shack up with me, I guess." He already knew the answer to that.

"Tempting. What would Sally think?"

"She'd think I have good taste."

He took her home without further argument. But as he turned onto her street, he finally decided what his next move would be. "Are you free for dinner tomorrow night? I mean a fancy steak dinner, all the trimmings."

"I'd love to. But you don't have to spend a lot of money. I'd be just as happy—"

"No way. We're going to Bremond's in Tyler."

"But that's so expensive."

"So? Anne, I'm not poor."

"But I thought—"

"You thought wrong. I need a steak dinner. With wine."

She smiled. "All right, that sounds nice."

And somehow, in the next twenty-four hours, he would come up with the magic words he needed. Maybe *I love you* would do the trick.

THE NEXT MORNING at breakfast, Anne could hardly focus on her father's ramblings about his early days as a lawyer. She was ready to see Wade again—more than ready. He'd become as addictive as morphine and a lot more fun.

At the same time, she was dreading it. She had delayed telling him about the baby for way too long. No matter what else was going on, tonight she had to tell him. They would be trapped in his truck during the long drive to Tyler, so he would be forced to listen to the whole story, including all her reasons for keeping the pregnancy a secret from him, weak though they were.

Her mother had said nothing about her going out with Wade yesterday. She'd said nothing about the fact that Anne had come home from the date looking...well, looking as if she'd been doing more than picking daisies. But Deborah had been watching her with more than her usual attention, giving her meaningful looks, then glancing at her father.

Deborah expected her to tell her father what was going on—before he heard it from someone else. Anne had so far failed to be honest with Wade—because she was terrified of what his reaction would be. She shouldn't make the same mistake with her dad.

"I'm going out to dinner tonight," she said as casually as she dared. "To Bremond's in Tyler."

Milton didn't look up from his *Wall Street Journal*. "Fancy place. Who are you going with?"

"Wade is taking me."

The paper came down. "Wade Hardison?"

"Yes."

"Are you out of your mind?"

"Perhaps. But I happen to think he's a very decent man."

"Decent? You've got to be kidding."

"Dad, you don't even know him."

"And I suppose you do?"

"I've gotten to know him pretty well, yes."

Milton looked to his wife. "Talk to her."

"I already tried."

"You knew about this and didn't tell me?"

"I wanted her to tell you."

Milton focused his penetrating stare at Anne. She resisted the urge to shrink back. "Are you paying for dinner?"

"Dad, of course not. He invited me, he'll pay."

"Humph. We'll see." He refocused on the paper, and she thought she was getting off easy, till he slammed the paper down on the table. "You're making a mistake with this boy," he declared, his eyes button-bright as he watched her, gauging her reaction. Milton never made a move without a purpose in mind, and in this case she guessed he wanted to see how emotional she would get. From that he could deduce how serious she was about Wade.

"That may be," she said calmly. "But I believe it's my mistake to make."

"I don't want you throwing away your future because of some adolescent crush."

"Oh, Milton," Deborah interrupted, "don't exaggerate. It's just a date, for heaven's sake. It's got to be dreary for Anne sitting in her room hour after hour with only her books for company. She's not a machine."

Anne was surprised by her mother coming to her

defense, and grateful. But Milton wasn't ready to let it go.

"Deborah, how can you take her side? She can't date Wade Hardison. It's unthinkable."

Anne tried not to bristle. He was concerned, she reminded herself. "It's very thinkable," she said calmly. "It's not only thinkable, it's doable. I'm already dating him."

"Don't you learn anything from your mistakes?"

She winced. Thinking of her baby as a "mistake" seemed so harsh. In truth, once she'd gotten over the shock, her pregnancy had secretly thrilled her. Though she'd never before thought of herself as a mother, falling into that role had been amazingly easy. She'd bought every book on pregnancy and babies and child care she could lay her hands on and had poured herself into the project. She'd endlessly debated breast feeding versus bottles, disposable diapers versus cloth, natural childbirth versus all the latest medical wizardry.

Her pregnancy had made her feel as if she'd been handed a sacred responsibility, and she'd taken it very, very seriously. Something that could make her feel so...miraculous could hardly be termed a mistake, even if nature had later decided that's exactly what it was.

"I didn't mean that," Milton said quickly, realizing he'd stepped over a line. "I just worry about your getting distracted from your real purpose."

"Dad, I've got my priorities straight, okay? I know I went a little nuts this summer, but I'm on track now. Listen to Mom, she's completely right. I need a break sometimes, and I like being with Wade."

"I understand your needing to be with people your own age, but why him?" Milton asked. "If you're going for one of the Hardison brothers, why not the doctor? Why does it have to be that black-sheep bull rider? Just mentioning his name makes old Pete spit."

"He's not a bull rider," Anne objected. "He's a calf roper. A champion, the best in the country."

"He's still a rodeo clown," Milton insisted, his voice rising. "Does he wear those sparkly red leather chaps?"

"Actually, his chaps are blue," Anne retorted, coming quickly to Wade's defense. "And he looks darn cute in them."

"Anne, where are your brains? A rodeo cowboy is not an appropriate—"

"All right, you two," Deborah said, cutting into the argument with her soft, reasoning voice. "Put your swords away. Milton, you're overreacting. Anne didn't say she wanted to marry the guy, just that she likes spending time with him. She's an adult, and she can spend time with whomever she wants."

"Thank you, Mom."

But Deborah wasn't done. "And you, young lady, I trust you won't give your father any reason to say 'I told you so.'"

So much for her mother seeing her as an adult.

Deflated, Milton left the table, muttering something about paying bills. Anne helped her mother clear the breakfast dishes and clean the kitchen. Deborah was unusually silent, and Anne wondered if her mother was merely concerned over her daughter's social life, or if it was something trickier.

Finally, when the kitchen was about as clean as it

could get, Deborah spoke. "So tell me, Anne, when exactly did you see Wade in his blue chaps?"

The air whooshed out of Anne's lungs. She hadn't given her mother enough credit. When her parents had pressed her a few months ago to know who the baby's father was, she had mumbled that it didn't matter, he was just someone she'd met at the rodeo. Apparently Deborah had filed that information away, and now she'd put the pieces together.

Anne leaned back against the kitchen counter and put her face in her hands, pressing back the tears that threatened behind her burning eyelids.

"Does he know?" her mother asked softly.

"No."

"You should probably tell him before he figures it out on his own. A lot of people know you were pregnant, his own father and brother among them."

"I've been struggling to find the courage. It's not that easy to tell a man—" She stopped herself. This wasn't something she needed to explain to her mother. "I'm going to tell him. Tonight." She would just have to push the words out of her mouth. Somehow.

"You're playing with fire, Anne. If you intend to string this boy along—"

"I'm not stringing him along. And for heaven's sake, he's not a boy. He's close to thirty. We're just spending time together, and we intend to continue."

"I never intended to stop you."

"But you think I'll get hurt."

"I think you might be the one to do the hurting. And believe me, Anne, that's not a position you want to be in."

AS WADE LAY IN BED that night, he realized he'd forgotten something. Anne had told him that his dad and

Jeff and Pete were worried about him and wanted to make amends. He'd filed the knowledge away for further scrutiny and possible action, but then he'd gotten all caught up in Kristin and his acrimonious exchange with Jonathan and then making love to Anne, which had blotted out all other thoughts.

The ball was in his court. If some members of his family wanted to open up a dialogue, he ought to respond.

First thing the next morning he called Jeff's office and managed to catch him before his first appointment arrived.

"Got a few minutes?" Wade asked.

"Sure, what's up?" Jeff sounded uneasy. They hadn't spoken since the day Wade had walked out of the hospital waiting room, intent on making a permanent exit from the family as well.

"Anne said you wanted to apologize," Wade said point-blank. "Well, you don't have to. All of us have done a pretty good job of laying blame and holding grudges, and I for one am sick to death of grudges. I want to move on."

"Amen to that." Jeff paused, and Wade sensed his brother's hesitancy. Then Jeff laughed nervously. "You want to have lunch later or what?"

"Sure, sounds good. Think you can drag Dad along?"

"I'll try."

After they decided on a time and place, Wade hung up, relieved. He could at least set things right, or as right as possible, with Jeff and his dad.

With a couple of hours to spare till lunch, he decided to pay a visit to the ranch. Five minutes with Pete was all he needed to gauge how serious the old man was about reconciliation.

Fortunately, Jonathan's truck wasn't parked in the driveway, which probably meant he was out with the cows. Eventually Wade would have to tangle with his oldest brother again, but one step at a time.

Sam greeted Wade at the door, lacking his usual enthusiasm. In fact, he peered cautiously at Wade, obviously not sure what to say.

Damn. If Jonathan had turned Wade's nephew against him, he didn't know what he would do.

"Hey, podner," Wade said. "Long time no see."

Sam didn't mince words. "Why'd you move out, Uncle Wade?" The little boy's earnest expression turned Wade's heart inside out. He hadn't realized his abrupt departure would worry Sam. Damn, he really needed some practice with this family obligation stuff.

Wade took Sam's hand and led him into the living room to sit down on the worn leather couch. How did he explain the complicated situation in a way Sam would understand?

He made a stab at it. "It was getting a little tense around here. Everyone was upset, with Kristin's operation and all, and we all needed some space."

"I didn't need any space."

Wade ruffled his hair. "You'll understand better when you get older. I missed you."

"I missed you, too. Daddy said it was your fault Kristin got hurt."

Wade took a deep breath, fighting the wave of resentment that threatened to engulf him. Somehow he managed to stay calm. "You could look at it that way. Your daddy told me to look after Kristin, and I didn't do a very good job of it. I don't know that I could have stopped her from falling off the bed if I'd been here instead of just Pete, but maybe I could have. I made a mistake in leaving the house when Kristin was sick, and I'm sorry for that. But you know I'd never, ever, do anything on purpose to hurt you or your sister, don't you?"

Sam nodded slowly.

"Just like that time you fell off your pony and got all scraped up. Your daddy felt terrible about that, like it was his fault, like maybe he shouldn't have been letting you ride that fast. But we all make choices, and some of 'em just don't work out like we planned. That's life. It's no good spending our whole lives blaming each other, or ourselves, when we're all doing the best we can."

Sam looked thoughtful. "Daddy's pretty mad at you."

"I know. I'm giving him some time to get over it. But really, I'm here to see you. And Pete. Has Grandpa Pete gotten over *his* cold?"

Sam nodded. "He's out in back working on the lawn mower."

Dang, the old man had more energy than lots of men half his age. "Let's go see him, then."

Pete was in the shed with the lawn mower in a hundred pieces, spread out over sheets of greasy newspaper—and he was cussing it like crazy.

"Hey, Pete. You're looking better than when I last saw you."

Pete grunted. "You may've thought I was at death's door, but you're not rid of me that easy. Here, you got better eyes than me. See if you can get this screw threaded right."

Wade was glad to have something to do with his hands. He remembered how, when he was little, he and Pete used to work on things together. Once they built a rabbit hutch, and Wade had always liked helping with his grandfather's various repair projects.

"Guess we was pretty hard on you," Pete said.

"Uh-huh."

"I know it wasn't your fault, little Kristy bumping her head. If anyone's to blame—"

"It was no one's fault. Kids have accidents. Can I see the Phillips screwdriver?"

Pete handed him the tool. "Where you been staying?"

"Sally Enderlin's place. I'm doing some work for her."

Pete's eyes lit up at the mention of Sally's name. "She oughtta sell."

"Farm's been in her family a long time."

"That's what she always says. You think she's doing okay? You know, making ends meet?"

"I think it's tough, but she's making it okay."

"Well, I'm glad you're helping her out, but you can move back here anytime you want. Jonathan might not like it, but it's still my house, and what I say goes."

Wade smiled. "I appreciate it. But I'll be leaving for Kansas City in a few days, anyway."

"You coming back?"

"I have every intention of it. Me and Traveler,

we're retiring after the American Royal. I'll be lookin' to buy some land, maybe build a house.''

''What do you have to buy land for? You got land. A third of this ranch belongs to you. Or it will when I kick.''

Wade dropped his screwdriver. ''What'd you say?''

''You heard me. A third of the Hardison Ranch has your name on it.''

''How come I'm just hearing about this?'' Wade figured he'd been disinherited long ago.

Pete shrugged. ''You didn't ask.''

He took a moment to absorb the news. Could he do it? Could he start up a horse-breeding operation right alongside Jonathan? He'd need to build his own facilities, he supposed, but it'd be worth it, not having to lay out cash for the acreage.

Did he really want to settle down in Cottonwood?

''What'll you do with yourself if you retire?'' Pete asked.

''I'm gonna breed horses. Fancy horses. And I'm gonna start a rodeo camp for city kids.'' There, he'd said it aloud. Just speaking his dream made it seem more real.

''So, what's the problem? You could take that acreage by the creek and put in trails for your fancy horses. And if you're keen to buy something, you could offer on Sally's place. She's already got a setup for horses. It butts right up against that creek property.''

''Any, um, particular reason you want Sally to sell?'' Wade asked, sensing an undercurrent.

''Oh, hell, I been trying for years to get Sally to

sell her place and marry me. Everyone knows that. Maybe she'd feel better if her land stayed in the family, more or less."

Wade was speechless. He'd always assumed it was Sally who was pining away and his grandfather who resisted. He couldn't quite imagine Pete being romantic. But the ranch sure could use a woman's touch.

"I'll think about it," Wade said, though he still wasn't sure where he'd settle. That partly depended on Anne. "And thanks, Granddad."

"Thank your dad. The whole ranch should've gone to him, but he didn't want it."

"How do you think Jonathan would deal with me setting up shop on Hardison land?" Wade asked.

"He'd like it a sight better than having you roam all over tarnation. Once he gets over this snit he's in."

"You think he *will* get over it?" Wade really wanted Pete's take on the situation. He probably knew Jonathan better than anyone.

"Hard to say. I thought you were the bullheaded one, but Jon's got a chip on his shoulder the size of a boulder. It'll take some time."

Wade suspected his brother's grudge went back before Kristin's accident. Jonathan had built up years of resentment over Wade abandoning his family responsibilities, but he'd kept it buried deep. It had taken this crisis with Kristin to bring all that bitterness bubbling to the surface. And once the cork blew, there was no pushing it back down.

It would take time for those wounds to heal. Unfortunately, time was one thing Wade didn't have on his side.

Chapter Twelve

Wade was first to arrive at Triple D Barbecue. He took a booth in back, and by the time he'd asked the waitress for a Sprite, his brother and father had arrived. They all ordered way more barbecue than any of them would eat, then stared at each other awkwardly.

"Did you know Kristin's coming home tomorrow?" Edward finally asked. "She's doing great."

"I'm glad to hear it."

They made small talk for a few minutes. Then Wade took a fortifying gulp of Sprite and made himself say what was on his mind. He looked at his father. "I assume Jeff filled you in on our conversation this morning."

Edward nodded.

"I meant what I said," Wade continued. "We could sit here and rehash old stuff. But I don't know what that would accomplish. Maybe we all learned something. I don't know. I just know I'm tired of walking on eggs. I want my family back—but am I going to have to keep proving that over and over?"

"Wade," Edward said, "as far as I'm concerned,

we're starting over. No baggage. Maybe you haven't lived the life I would have picked for you, but it was obviously what you were meant to do. It's time we acknowledged the man you are and stopped mourning the one we thought you should be."

Wade looked at Jeff, who nodded in agreement. "But I just have one bone to pick, first," Jeff said. "If family is so important to you, why are you leaving again? Nothing's going to be solved if you take off."

"I thought things *were* solved."

"He means between you and Jonathan," Edward said. "I know things are difficult between you and Jon, but you can't work them out if you're not here. Running is not the answer."

Wade smiled and shook his head at the melodrama his brother and father had created. "I'm not running. I have to compete in Kansas City next week. There's a hundred-thousand-dollar purse in the balance."

"And then...you're coming back?" Edward asked, looking surprised.

Wade nodded. "If I do well at the American Royal, and I have every reason to believe I will, I'll win the national championship. Then I'm quitting rodeo—at least the professional circuit. I'm settling down to raise horses."

Jeff and Edward stared at him with twin sets of shocked eyes. Finally his father spoke. "You're going to *ranch?*"

"No, not ranch. I'll be a horse breeder and trainer."

"What the hell's the difference?" Jeff wanted to know. "You have some land and a bunch of livestock on the hoof. You breed it, raise it, sell it."

Jeff obviously knew nothing about the world of high-end horse breeding. "It's a matter of scale," Wade said. "You don't deal with vast herds. You focus on one animal at a time. And you sell it to someone who'll ride it rather than kill it and eat it."

Edward smiled. "Interesting distinction." He nodded toward the plate of ribs in front of Wade.

"This sudden interest of yours in settling down," Jeff said. "Would it have something to do with Anne?"

He'd been hoping they wouldn't have to discuss Anne. No matter what Jeff's good intentions were, Wade feared his brother would never believe he was good enough for Anne.

"I've been thinking about retiring for a while, now," Wade answered. "Being with Anne made me want to commit to the idea, that's all."

"Then you and Anne—" Edward looked confused. "You're serious?"

Wade didn't know how to answer that question. He was serious as hell, but he couldn't speak for Anne. "I'll know more about that after tonight," he said cryptically.

WADE WAS EARLY when he picked Anne up. He'd washed and waxed his truck, she noticed as he drove up into the driveway. It looked pretty good. She was watching from the living-room window, where she'd been for half an hour.

When Wade opened the door and climbed out, however, he outshone the truck by several kilowatts. She'd never seen him wear anything but jeans. Tonight, he had on a pair of dark-gray slacks, a white button-down shirt and a silk tie. He'd gotten a haircut.

Except for the dress cowboy boots, he could have looked at home in any boardroom in America. She did not have to worry about taking him to the company Christmas party. He would be the envy of every out-of-shape, pale-skinned male lawyer, and the target of every hot-to-trot woman.

She hurried to the door, not wanting either of her parents to beat her there. For a few moments she and Wade just stared at each other. Did he like what he saw? She'd dressed with exceptional care in a clingy, long-sleeved black cocktail dress with a plunging neckline and an almost nonexistent back. She'd put her hair up in a twist, leaving several strands loose to give it the tousled, careless look she saw on the covers of fashion magazines.

She'd put diamond studs in her ears and a matching necklace around her neck, the pendant flirting with her cleavage. She'd even painted her nails a dark amber and applied lipstick to match. When she'd assessed her appearance in the mirror, she'd seen no trace of Anne, the stodgy almost-lawyer. Nor had she seen Annie, the flirtatious, outrageous rodeo hussy.

The woman who'd looked back at her was sexy and sophisticated. Yet another side of her personality? If she didn't watch out, someone was going to make a TV movie about her multiple-personality disorder. Or maybe she just hadn't figured out who she wanted to be when she grew up.

Wade apparently liked the end result of her grooming, because he couldn't stop staring at her. "You're gorgeous. You're the prom date I never had."

She smiled back. "I didn't go to the prom, either. I was a squirrelly teenager."

"Me, too. I didn't seem to fit in anywhere. Even on the rodeo circuit I was something of an oddity. I didn't really feel comfortable there till I was old enough to stop forging my father's signature on the competition applications."

Anne felt a presence behind her. She turned to find her mother hovering, looking uncertain.

"Wade," Deborah said with a nod and a cautious smile. "You look very nice. Would you like to come in?"

"No, thank you, Mrs. Chatsworth. Our reservations are for seven-thirty in Tyler."

Anne breathed a sigh of relief. She didn't think she could endure five minutes with her parents and Wade all in the same room. Milton would pull out all the stops. He would do his subtle best to point out Wade's flaws and shortcomings without making it obvious he had negative intentions.

Anne grabbed her purse from the coat tree. "We better go," she said inanely.

"When should I expect you home?" Deborah asked.

Anne gave her a dark look.

"I know, I know. You're all grown-up. Is there any particular time I should become concerned?"

"If it's going to be very late, I'll call," Anne said noncommittally, though perhaps her mother's concern was well-founded. After she told Wade her secret, he might dump her out on the highway and make her hitchhike home.

Still, tonight was the night, no matter what.

She and Wade made their escape. Wade chuckled as he opened the door and gallantly assisted Anne into the truck.

"What's so funny?"

"Your mom. She's like a mother cat protecting her kitten from the bulldog next door."

"She worries."

"I thought your father would be the one giving me the third degree," Wade said once he'd slid behind the wheel.

"He was apparently boycotting the front-door scene."

"They're really not happy about your going out with me."

"I told you, they'd be concerned no matter who I was going out with. My father thinks it's interfering with my whole future, that I should be focused on the bar and the job search and nothing else."

"You have to have some balance in your life."

Balance. She did need it, she realized. She always fell to one extreme or the other. The whole reason she went to the rodeo was because she'd been focusing too hard on her studies. Then once she was there, she forgot completely about school and fell headfirst into that alternate Annie persona.

When she was pregnant, she'd become obsessed with being a mother and had shoved lawyering to the side. When she'd lost her baby, she'd thrown herself right back into the future-lawyer business.

"I seem to have a problem with the whole balance thing," she said. "I guess I'm a wee bit obsessive."

"I haven't sensed any obsession where I'm concerned,'' Wade said, sounding almost aggrieved. ''Not lately.''

''That's because you don't see inside my head. Outwardly I'm still studying and fielding job offers and researching different cities where I might live, but inside I'm thinking about you constantly.''

He shot her a playful grin. ''That's what people do when they fall in love.''

Anne held her breath. Should she argue that she wasn't in love with Wade? Or should she just admit it? If he knew she loved him, maybe the other confessions she intended to make tonight would be easier to accept.

He kept his eyes on the road. ''No denial, counselor?''

''I'm deliberating my rebuttal.''

''That's what I was afraid of. For the record, I can't stop thinking about you, either. You can take that to its logical conclusion.''

The implication thrilled her far more than it should have. Wade being in love with her—and willing to admit it in his own oblique way—complicated the hell out of her task for the evening. She wasn't just going to make him angry. She was going to disillusion him, maybe really hurt him.

He was most certainly going to hurt her.

Wade stepped neatly away from the subject of love, probably because she hadn't responded in an encouraging way. He commented on how green the landscape was, despite the fact it was almost November, and how he'd forgotten how beautiful the East Texas countryside around Cottonwood was. He kept up a steady stream of inconsequential conversation, and she barely managed to hold up her end.

Why had she delayed so long telling Wade the truth? If she'd done it that first afternoon, when they met at the fair, she might have stood a chance of salvaging something with him. But she just hadn't realized how badly she would want to do that.

Bremond's, an excellent steak house patronized by people from all over East Texas, bustled with activity. Despite the crowd, the hostess seated them immediately at a quiet, candlelit table in a curtained alcove.

"I haven't been here in a long time," Wade said, "not since I was eight or nine years old. It hasn't changed much."

"Still that huge longhorn head on the wall."

"That thing used to scare me to death. Guess I knew even when I was a little kid I didn't want to be a rancher and herd those things around."

"Oh, no, you just want to ride *really* angry ones, bareback."

"I don't do that much anymore. You have to have a spine like a Slinky to be good at it. I chose roping 'cause the calves aren't that scary."

Anne smiled and shook her head. She didn't believe Wade was afraid of anything—except maybe losing his family for good. He acted as if it wasn't that important, but she knew it was.

She ordered the first thing she saw on the menu that didn't sound like half a cow on a plate. All through dinner she mentally rehearsed how she would bring up the subject of her pregnancy. At one point Wade asked her if something was wrong. Apparently, he'd noticed she wasn't delivering a barrage of scintillating conversation.

"I'm a little tired, I guess," she said.

"You seem preoccupied."

"That, too."

"Is it something you want to talk about?"

She swallowed. He'd given her the perfect opening. *Say it. Just say it.* "There is something I need to discuss with you."

"If you're going to dump me, do it now," he said bluntly.

She shook her head. "It's not that at all." She wouldn't have to dump him. He would dump her.

She put down her silverware, unable to eat any more of her fillet, which she hadn't tasted, anyway. She blotted her mouth. The words she'd mentally rehearsed earlier were perversely absent from her brain. How was she supposed to begin?

"I'm glad to hear that," Wade said. "I didn't ask you to dinner at this special place just for no reason. I have some things to say, and I was afraid you'd leave town without warning and I wouldn't get the chance."

"I wouldn't leave without saying goodbye."

"Still, time is getting away from us. This is important."

A feeling of foreboding settled on Anne's shoulders. What was going on here?

"I know you have to leave Cottonwood. I know you have to take advantage of the fantastic opportunities you've worked so hard for, and I wouldn't dream of asking you to change your whole life plan just to suit me."

If only he would ask her to, she might. She was so unsure of what she wanted now.

"Still, I want to be with you, Anne. Now, a week from now, months, years from now. I know those two things seem hard to reconcile, but I feel like somehow we can do it."

He reached down and picked up something that was next to his chair, then held it out to her—a velvet-covered box.

Anne's head swam, and she thought she might pass out. Where had that box come from?

"It's not an engagement ring," he said softly. "So you can stop looking like a frog that's just been gigged."

She clutched the box, scared to death to open it.

"I know this is kind of sudden. Ordinarily I wouldn't want to move so fast. But we don't have all kinds of time. If I didn't state my case, you'd be gone before I knew it. Open the box."

She did. Inside was a lovely necklace with an emerald surrounded by diamonds, all set in swirling gold. It wasn't huge, but it sparkled and winked at her.

"This was my mother's," Wade said, his voice thick. "When she knew she was dying, she gave each of her kids a piece of her jewelry. She said I should give this necklace to that one special woman."

Anne shook her head as tears pressed against her closed eyelids. Oh, God. Oh, no, he couldn't mean this. She wasn't special. She'd withheld the news of his child to him. She'd planned to raise it without him. How would he ever forgive her for something like that?

"I know you're not in any position to make commitments," he continued. "I'm not asking you to marry me. But I thought, as long as you have my mother's necklace, there's something between us, like a promise. A promise that we have a future."

For a few minutes, Anne let herself absorb what Wade had said. A future. Was it possible? She hadn't let herself think about it, not in any detail. Now he was laying it out for her, a gaudy temptation, the apple on the Tree of Knowledge. Beautiful, tempting, but ultimately not for her to have.

Quietly she closed the box and handed it back to him. "You should give this to your wife, when you have one."

He shook his head. "It's yours. I've never even considered giving it to any other woman. You're the one it was meant for. I love you, Anne. Even if we can't be together now, someday we'll work it out—if we want it bad enough. Someday I want to marry you. I want us to have kids together—little Sams and Kristins of our very own."

Anne gasped, dropping the jeweler's box. She'd have survived this night, somehow, if he hadn't mentioned children. She slid out of her chair and grabbed her purse. Her fight-or-flight mechanism was in full gear, and all she could think about was fleeing.

"I have to go."

"What?"

"I'm feeling ill." Which wasn't a lie. The beef she'd eaten sat like a lump of lead in her stomach, and she felt as if she might lose it any second. She turned and left the alcove, needing to get outside and breathe some fresh air.

She made it all the way to the truck, but the door was locked. She had nowhere else to go, no way to get home unless she called her parents to come get her, which was not a good idea. So she waited, knowing Wade would come after her in moments. She would have to come up with some explanation for her deplorable behavior.

She leaned against the truck, put her face in her hands and wept.

WADE FOUND HER LIKE THAT, crying noisy tears, and his heart felt as if it was being ripped to ribbons. Talk about your all-time disastrous reactions to a romantic overture. Was a future with him really that horrifying? She could have just said, "No, thanks."

He let her be for a minute or two, but the sight of her crying was tearing him up inside. He couldn't just let her bawl her eyes out like that. With a resigned sigh, he walked up to her, his feet heavy, and handed her a handkerchief. Lord knew what had possessed him to stick one in his pocket as he dressed, but he was glad he had.

She took the handkerchief and mopped at her face, then blew her nose. He sidled up next to her. "Forget I mentioned anything about the future, okay? Obviously, it was a stupid idea."

That just made her cry harder. Jeez, he couldn't say anything right. Figuring words were useless, he opened her door and practically boosted her into the truck. The sooner he got her back to her house, the sooner she could get away from him, which seemed to be what she wanted.

He drove faster than he should have down the highway toward Cottonwood, eager now to end this ill-fated date. He just didn't understand women. Didn't they like it when men made fools of themselves? Even if she felt nothing for him, she could have been flattered by his declaration and his mushy, sentimental gift.

Then it occurred to him. Maybe her tears meant she *did* feel something for him, but for whatever reason she couldn't accept his love, and that's what made her cry. The thought didn't exactly cheer him up. His ego didn't worry him as much as his cheerless future.

When her tears had diminished to an occasional sniffle, Wade risked asking her something. "Are you in love with someone else?"

She gave a little bark of a laugh. "I wish it was that easy. No."

"Are you dying of some terrible disease?"

She paused for a moment, as if considering that one. "No."

"Have you made your final vows of chastity to a convent?"

"No."

"Are you...already married?" That's the one he really feared for her to answer. It had never occurred to him, until now, that she might have a husband tucked away somewhere, the result of a foolish young marriage she felt obligated to continue with.

"Definitely not."

"Then could you tell me why you fell apart back there?"

"Not now."

"Some time soon? You know, you've just given

my ego another near-fatal bruising. You're pretty good at that."

"I don't mean to. I just wasn't expecting..."

"I surprised myself, too." He'd only meant to give her the necklace so she would know she was special to him, not tell her he loved her and wanted her to bear his children.

"Are you breaking up with me? I thought you weren't going to break up with me."

"Please, Wade, I just can't talk about this right now."

He guessed that was a yes, despite her earlier reassurance that she wasn't dumping him.

When he pulled into her parents' driveway, Anne couldn't escape his truck fast enough. She didn't even thank him for dinner. She just bolted for her front door.

Wade sat there in his truck, engine idling, for a long while. Several times he started to drive away, but something stopped him. This wasn't right. Something odd was going on here. The Anne Chatsworth he thought he knew was not a flighty, emotional mess. If she simply hadn't wanted to tie herself down to a long-distance relationship with him, she would have told him, probably using a lot of big words, all very sensible.

There was something she hadn't told him. And, damn it, he was going to find out what it was.

He switched off the engine just as the front door opened again. He thought it was Anne, and his hopes rose, only to be dashed again. The figure emerging from the house was tall, beefy and very male.

Milton Chatsworth.

Wade didn't mind admitting that Anne's father intimidated him. But this wasn't a fight he was willing to back down from. His whole future was at stake. If Anne wouldn't tell him what was going on, maybe Milton would.

Wade got out of the truck and faced Milton, who came at him like a freight train.

"What the hell did you say to her?" Milton demanded.

Chapter Thirteen

Wade decided the situation called for total honesty. "I told her how much I cared for her," he said. "And that I wanted to be with her."

"So you told her to give up her law career so she can bum around—"

"No, not at all. I wouldn't ask that of her. I just wanted her to think about a future with me. Not tomorrow, not next week, but when we're both established."

"Established doing *what?*" Milton boomed. "You're a nomadic rodeo cowboy!"

"I'm retiring. I'm going into horse breeding." He felt no need to justify himself further. The problem was Anne, not himself. "I love your daughter, Mr. Chatsworth. Someday I want to marry her. I want to have children with her."

Some of the fight went out of Milton. "You told her that?"

"Yes. I don't understand why she became upset. If she doesn't feel the same about me, that's one thing. I can handle rejection. But there's something else going on."

"Oh, hell, why didn't I figure this out before?" Milton said, talking more to himself than Wade. "She said it was at the rodeo."

"Pardon me?"

He skewered Wade with a piercing stare. "You're the son of a bitch that got her pregnant."

For a few seconds Wade couldn't breathe. Then he was filled with an irrational sense of joy. Anne, pregnant with his child? He couldn't imagine anything better. But how could she know, this soon? Less than two weeks had passed since their encounter at the creek.

He thought back to Anne's demeanor at dinner. An unplanned pregnancy would explain her agitated state and her distress when he mentioned children. Lord knew a baby would wreak havoc on her career plans. She was probably in shock. But surely she wanted to keep it. If she didn't, she wasn't the woman he'd fallen in love with.

"Anne is pregnant?" Wade asked Milton, just to be sure he hadn't misunderstood.

Before Milton could answer, Deborah Chatsworth appeared at the door. "Milton!"

Milton turned, startled by the strident tone in Deborah's voice.

"Do not say another word. This is not our affair."

"I want to see Anne," Wade insisted. "If she's pregnant with my child, I have a right to know."

Milton put a hand to his head. "Oh, dear God, this is a mess." He shrugged, defeated. "Deborah, I think you'd better convince your daughter to set this young man straight."

Anne appeared from behind her mother, looking

frail and unsteady. Wade wanted to go right to her, throw his arms around her, tell her how happy he was. He loved kids. He'd always wanted some of his own.

But Anne did not look as if she would welcome an overt gesture of affection from him. She had her arms crossed, her feet pressed firmly together, her head bowed. Maybe she was just cold, but he didn't think so.

Deborah stepped toward her husband and took his arm. "Come on, Milton. Anne, we'll be upstairs if you need anything." They went into the house, leaving the door open and Anne standing just outside the threshold.

Wade went forward, close enough he could see Anne's tearstained face. Her nose was red, her makeup smeared everywhere, but she was still the most beautiful woman he'd ever seen. The mother of his child.

"Anne?" he said cautiously. "Is it true?"

"Can we go inside?" she said in a thready voice.

"Sure." He followed her into the house, through the living room and dining room, and into the kitchen.

"Do you want something to drink?" She went to the refrigerator, opened it and peered inside.

"Anne, I want you to talk to me. Are you pregnant?"

She turned back toward him, her face so filled with pain he could feel it physically, himself, pinching his chest. "No."

He sagged with disappointment and confusion. "Then what—"

"I was pregnant this summer. I had a miscarriage when I was almost four months along."

The reality hit him like a sledgehammer to the head. She'd seemed pale and a little weak when he'd first seen her at the Autumn Daze. He'd also thought she'd gained a few pounds, which would make sense. No wonder everyone had been so protective of her—Jeff, his dad, her parents.

"Am I right to assume it was mine?"

She nodded.

He'd almost been a father. His chest contracted again, harder this time. Then a more painful reality hit him. "You weren't going to tell me."

"I tried calling you when I first found out."

"You must not have tried very hard."

She slumped into a chair at the breakfast table. "No. It was a token effort. I didn't know how you'd react. I thought you'd be angry. It just seemed like the last thing in the world a guy like you would want was a kid to tie you down."

"Then you don't know me very well."

"Back then I didn't know you well at all. We'd spent one weekend together. The subject of children never came up, even in the abstract. Now that I know you better, I realize how wrong I was."

"But you still didn't tell me. Jeez, Anne, did everyone know but me?"

"I guess a lot of people did know, though that wasn't my choice. And no one knew you were the father, not even Jeff, and he was my doctor. My parents only just now put two and two together. And I was going to tell you. But it was just so hard. I never could find the right moment. I know I should have. I'm sorry. And I'm sorry for falling apart tonight."

Wade was overwhelmed. He didn't have any idea

what to say, how to react. Finally he asked the only question that came to mind. "Were you going to raise the child? Or give it up?"

"Raise it, of course. I could never give away a child I'd carried."

"But you had no qualms about denying the child a father."

"I didn't know you then! I was afraid you wouldn't care. I was afraid you'd think I'd trapped you on purpose, that I was after you for child support or...or..."

He couldn't listen to this. He'd never been so angry with anyone, not even Jonathan. He had to get away from Anne before he did something he might regret. Without another word, he turned and left.

ANNE COULD DO NOTHING but shake for a few minutes after Wade left. After that passed, it got worse. She spent almost an hour thinking she was going to throw up, but that passed, too. Finally she just went numb. Drawing her knees up to her chest, she wrapped her arms around her legs and sat there staring out the window toward the blackness of the lake. She willed her mind to stay empty, for to think about anything that had just happened was too painful to bear.

Her mother found her that way some time later. Anne wasn't sure how long she'd been sitting there, but her body was racked with cramps.

Thankfully Deborah didn't say a word. She just guided Anne to her feet and gently led her upstairs. Once in her room, she undressed Anne as if she were a child again, threw a cotton nightgown over her head and pulled back the covers on the bed.

Anne impulsively threw her arms around her mother. ''Oh, Mom, what have I done?''

''Don't think about it now, darling,'' Deborah said. ''You'll feel better in the morning.''

Anne doubted that. But at least the suspense was over. Wade was furious, and he wanted nothing to do with her.

WADE WAS BESIDE HIMSELF with anger, and he stayed that way for the next week. Fortunately, Traveler's recovery had dramatically accelerated, and focusing all of his energy on his horse helped him to keep thoughts of Anne and her betrayal at bay.

Wade was able to exercise Traveler gently at first. Then, when he showed no signs of pain or relapse, they worked a bit harder. They went to the livestock-exchange arena and practiced on some calves, and Traveler was as excited and full of energy as he'd been in his youth.

''You're not ready for the pasture yet, are you, buddy?'' Wade crooned after a particularly long practice session. He gave Traveler a thorough rubdown, which the stallion loved. Traveler went into some kind of altered state while he was being groomed, as if he was meditating.

Doc Chandler had given the okay for Traveler to compete, so Wade called the American Royal people and told them to put him back on the slate. He packed up his things, which didn't take long. The sooner he got out of this town, the less likely he'd be to succumb to temptation and see Anne.

If only she hadn't deceived him. If only she'd trusted him enough to share her pregnancy with him.

With trust they could have formed an unbreakable bond. He wouldn't have enjoyed the firsthand experience of losing a child, but he and Anne could have helped each other through it. He could have been a source of great strength for her.

Instead she'd shut him out.

He could almost understand and forgive her for not telling him at first. He'd given her no clue that he would be a good father, that he would welcome a child. But after they'd gotten back together here in Cottonwood, her lack of honesty was unforgivable.

He realized he'd been thinking about Anne for five whole minutes without collapsing in pain. He was going to get through this. He might not ever get over it, but he would survive.

The day before his scheduled departure, he went to the ranch to say goodbye to Pete and the kids—and Jonathan, if his brother would talk to him. But Jon was nowhere to be found when Wade got there.

"I told him you were coming," Pete said letting Wade into the welcome warmth of the living room. "He lit out of here like his tail was on fire."

"Daddy doesn't have a tail," Kristin said. She was up and around now, if a bit slower-paced than she'd been before the accident. Still, her improvement was gratifying to witness.

"Are you sure he doesn't have one?" Pete groused. "He's acting like a—"

"Pete..." Wade warned. Whether he agreed with Pete or not, he didn't want anyone speaking ill of Jonathan in front of his children.

"Yeah, yeah. Kristin, why don't you go get that new Barbie to show your uncle Wade? And dress her up in that fancy ball gown.'' Kristin immediately departed, thinking this a great idea, and Pete chuckled. ''That'll keep her busy a few minutes, anyway. Come on out to the patio. I'm in the middle of grilling.''

''Something you wanted to talk about?'' Wade followed his grandfather out the back door, where the barbecue grill gave an enticing, smoky aroma.

''Yeah. I want to know how Anne feels about your running off to Kansas City.'' Pete picked up a set of tongs and turned the steaks. ''I mean, maybe it's none of my business—''

''It isn't,'' Wade said, though he knew that wouldn't stop Pete.

''—but I thought you two lovebirds would want to spend as much time together as possible afore she takes off to New York.''

''New York?'' Wade asked, seizing on any news of Anne despite his vow to stop obsessing about her. ''She's chosen the firm in New York?''

Pete looked at him quizzically. ''You're asking me?''

''Anne and I aren't exactly on speaking terms anymore.''

Pete's jaw dropped.

As Wade debated how to explain, Jeff and Edward came out the patio door.

''Anybody home?'' Edward called.

Pete, quickly overcoming his catatonia, whomped Wade on the head with his tongs. ''This bonehead son of yours already lost our Anne. Just when I was beginning to think he might be good enough for her.''

''You lost her?'' Jeff asked. ''You mean she

dumped you? Or did you break up with her? I thought there might be a compatibility problem, but—''

''Jeff, pipe down,'' Edward said. ''So what did happen?'' he asked Wade, as if they all had a perfect right to know. Wade was surprised they hadn't heard the news.

And maybe they did deserve to know. Anne *was* like family to them, and there had been enough deception. He would let the truth speak for itself. ''I assume you know she was pregnant last summer.'' Hell, it seemed everyone knew but Wade.

All three of the other men nodded.

''What you probably don't know is that I was the father.'' His revelation was greeted by stunned silence. Finally Jeff found his voice.

''How could that be?''

''We met up in Dallas.'' Wade explained about the rodeo, how Anne was there to blow off steam and how he didn't even know she was Anne Hardison from Cottonwood, because he hadn't seen her in thirteen years. ''I don't know how she could have kept it a secret from me, but it destroyed any trust we had.''

Jeff had gone noticeably pale. He exchanged a look with Edward. ''Did Anne tell you the, um, other part?''

Wade stared back blankly. ''What other part?''

''Oh, boy.''

''What, 'Oh, boy'? What other part?''

Jeff shook his head. ''It's not for me to discuss. You'll have to talk to Anne.''

''You mean she's keeping more secrets from me?''

Jeff and their dad adamantly refused to say anything else about it.

But Wade had no intention of seeing Anne again. She could keep her secrets. They had no bearing on him anymore.

ANNE'S PARENTS had been particularly kind to her after her blowup with Wade. They'd made no demands of her. They hadn't urged her to study or make a decision regarding employment. The most they had done was invite her to participate in low-stress activities with them, such as gardening and riding around in the boat. For the first week or so she'd fantasized that Wade would cool down and come back to her and they could talk. But a few days later she'd heard through the grapevine that Wade had left town. Then she'd simply let go of her romantic dreams about Wade and drifted.

It had done her a world of good not to worry about anything. She didn't think there'd ever been a time in her life she hadn't worried about something.

Another week drifted by in a haze.

Finally Milton couldn't stand it any longer. He approached her where she was reading in the sunroom.

"Mind if I join you?"

"Of course not, Dad." She patted the chair next to hers, which he took.

"Any idea when you're going to resume your life? Not that I'm pushing. I want you to take your time. After you lost the baby, you didn't grieve long enough, according to your mother. She says that's why the breakup with Wade hurt so badly—because you still needed to grieve."

Anne wasn't used to her father talking about personal matters. She knew it was difficult for him, and she appreciated the effort he was making. "I don't know how to resume my life," she admitted. "I've got all these nice offers from great law firms, and yet I can't seem to make myself commit to any of them."

"It's common to hesitate at this time. Everyone's afraid of making the wrong choice. But making the wrong choice is better than no choice at all. These offers won't be around forever."

"I know. Tomorrow I'll make a definite choice, okay? I'll call whomever I choose and commit." Then at least she would have something to occupy her time—finding a place to live, moving, signing up to take the bar exam in February, obtaining study materials for the state portion of whatever state she chose.

But she couldn't face any of those decisions today. Tomorrow she would be stronger, she promised herself.

When evening rolled around, Anne did what she'd done every night recently—she parked herself on the sofa in the den and channel surfed. She'd never been a couch potato, but now she could understand the appeal.

So many channels, so many means of escape. Gardening channel...home-decorating channel...cooking channel...rodeo chan—

Anne had almost clicked right over it. Rodeo? Must be on a sports channel. And what rodeo would be on national television except the biggest one going on right now, the American Royal in Kansas City—live?

The barrel racers were competing. Would Wade be

hanging around to congratulate the winner or console the loser? Or was he preparing for his own event later?

She shouldn't watch. She should turn off the TV and go to bed with a good book. But she couldn't make herself hit the off button. She was hungry for some glimpse of Wade, any little piece of him to add to her store of bittersweet memories. And maybe she wanted evidence that he hurt as badly as she did. She didn't relish the vengeful part of herself, but she acknowledged it and took what comfort it could offer.

Anne made herself a bag of popcorn and settled down to wait.

WADE FELT only a little nervous. He and Traveler had been competing well all week. They'd been in "the zone"—they couldn't do anything wrong. He had already qualified for the finals on Saturday, but a few more points wouldn't hurt him.

"You guys are hot!"

Wade looked up from where he sat on a hay bale in Traveler's stall, inspecting his pigging strings—the leather strips used to tie the calf. A buxom blonde stood on a rail of the stall door, rubbing Traveler's nose. The horse barely tolerated it, because his nose was ticklish, but he was a good sport.

"My friend Lori told me you're a national champion."

"Not yet. Soon."

"Gonna get you a big gold belt buckle, huh?"

"God willin' and the creek don't rise." He summoned a smile for the woman, who was very young...and very friendly. Oh, Lord, he recognized the look in her eye. She was a buckle bunny looking to make a conquest. His experience with Annie had cured him forever of one-night stands. But this gal was a winsome thing, and a little female company couldn't hurt. Maybe it would help wash memories of Anne from his brain, at least for a while.

"What's your name?" Wade asked.

"Wendy. And you're Wade, I already knew that. And your horse is Traveler. That's a nice name, Traveler. How'd you come up with it?"

"General Robert E. Lee came up with it first, for his horse. I just stole it out of a history book. Say, how'd you like to go out tonight and spend some of my prize money?"

"I'd love it." Her smile got bigger. "I know a place not far from here where they grill a steak bigger than your head."

"Okay, you're on. I got work to do now, but let's hook up later."

"It's a date." She fluttered her fingers in a flirtatious wave and sauntered off. Through the slats in the stall door he could see her hips swaying provocatively.

They did nothing for him.

Wade knew he ought to be happily looking forward to his rendezvous with Wendy. Instead he felt a little depressed. He used to enjoy the game a lot. He liked having women seek him out. He liked flirting with them and sometimes taking them to bed. But Anne had ruined all that for him.

He even felt guilty just making dinner plans with another woman, which was ridiculous. He and Anne were finished. She had betrayed his trust, and he owed her no loyalty. But he felt guilty all the same, as if he was cheating.

Part of his life—the macho, king-of-the-rodeo stuff—was over. He was moving into a new phase—the stable, settled-down, horse-breeding stage. He supposed he was allowed to mourn.

Growing up was hell.

He dismissed all thoughts of Wendy as the time drew near for his ride. Traveler pranced around, nostrils flared, snorting at the smell of sawdust and mares. Maybe he smelled the calves' fear, too.

"Take it easy, buddy," Wade said as he and Traveler took their positions, ready to shoot across the starting line when the signal was given. "Pace yourself. You don't have to go all-out. This one's for free."

With one final pat to the horse's neck, he gave the signal that he was ready. The calf was released, and Traveler bolted forward, all muscle and adrenaline.

The ride didn't feel right from the beginning. The stupid calf didn't run straight but cut to the right. Wade pulled Traveler up short to keep the two animals from colliding. Traveler stumbled, and his left foreleg gave out. They crashed to the ground, and Traveler rolled on top of Wade just as Wade struck the dirt. He saw stars, then, nothing.

ANNE'S WHOLE BODY went rigid as she watched the spectacle of Wade's fall in what seemed like slow motion. She must have cried out, though she didn't remember doing it, because her mother rushed into the room a few moments later.

"Anne, what's wrong? Are you all right?"

"I'm fine, but—" She gestured helplessly toward the TV screen, which showed a crowd of people surrounding man and horse, neither of which had immediately regained his feet.

"What's going on?" Deborah asked, still confused. Then they showed Wade's ill-fated run in excruciatingly slow motion while the announcer commented on exactly what he thought had happened. Anne could see Wade's head bounce against the ground as he hit, saw the horse land on Wade's lower body.

Deborah took a couple of steps closer to the TV, squinting at the screen. "Is that...?"

"Yes."

Deborah said nothing more, just silently reached for and squeezed Anne's hand as they both watched Traveler stumble yet again, his leg crumpling under him, then Wade's attempt to jump clear. But he wasn't fast enough, no matter how many times they replayed it.

The TV coverage went back to real time, and Anne took a gasping breath when she saw Wade get to his feet and wave to the crowd, refusing the stretcher that had been wheeled out for him.

"He's okay!" Deborah cried.

Wade did appear to be walking and talking. But Traveler—the poor horse was thrashing about, panicked and unable to regain his feet. The cameras cut away from the pitiful sight and went to commercial.

"Poor Traveler," Anne said. "Oh, Mom, I have to go to him."

Deborah looked at her in confusion. "The horse?"

"No, to Wade."

Deborah sucked in a breath. "Wade is all right, dear."

"But his horse—you don't understand. He loves that horse like a child. What if they have to destroy him? Wade will be distraught."

Deborah just shook her head. "So you're going to..."

"Kansas City."

"Tonight?"

"Yes."

Deborah firmed her mouth, then seemed to come to a decision. "I'll make the air reservations. You go pack."

Anne gave her mother a hug for understanding and not asking too many questions. They watched the TV long enough to see Traveler walk out of the arena—though his front leg, dangling at an odd angle, was obviously broken.

"Hardison is being looked at by a doctor," the announcer said. "But word is he just has a few bumps and bruises. His horse, though, the legendary Traveler, is out of competition for the foreseeable future."

"That's too bad," the color announcer added. "Hardison has led all year long in the race for the national calf-roping championship. Without a good score in the final round, he's lost his chance at that hefty purse."

More bad news, Anne thought as she ran upstairs to pack. She threw a change of clothes and a toothbrush into an overnight case. By the time she came downstairs dressed for travel, Deborah had a page of information printed out from Milton's computer.

"There's a flight at midnight from DFW," she

said. "You'll have to hurry, but don't drive too fast. If you miss it, there's another at two."

No way she would miss it, Anne thought. "I won't drive too fast. What will you tell Dad?" Her father had slept peacefully through the uproar.

"Nothing will surprise him at this point. I'll tell him the truth. He'll be relieved you're finally doing something. Your inaction was about to kill him."

"I'm moving now. I can't imagine why I didn't do this before, why I didn't go after what I wanted before. Does it always take a crisis to bring me to my senses?"

"Dear, some people never come to their senses. Get going, now. And be careful."

Anne gave her mother another quick hug before heading out to her car. She threw her one small bag into the passenger seat of the Mustang and took off.

IT WAS CLOSE TO THREE in the morning by the time Anne handed over her credit card to the rental-car company at Kansas City International Airport. They didn't have a compact available, so she grabbed a luxury car and didn't even blink at the cost. Nothing mattered now except finding Wade. The woman at the rental-car desk gave Anne a map and directions to the American Royal Arena.

"But it's all closed down this time of night," the clerk said. "And if you don't already have a hotel reservation, lots of luck. The whole city is full up 'cause of the rodeo."

"I hope I won't need a hotel," Anne replied.

Chapter Fourteen

Wade lay in his bunk, aching from his scalp to his toes. He had a sprained ankle and multiple bruises, possibly a broken rib, not to mention a concussion. But that was nothing compared to what poor Traveler had suffered.

He heard a noise outside his trailer and immediately became more alert. A reporter had pestered him all evening, wanting to know how it felt to lose all hope of winning the championship when he'd been so close. Normally Wade showed endless patience with the press, even when he wasn't in the mood. Those reporters had a job to do, too. But this guy had crossed over *annoying* right to *abrasive.* Wade wouldn't put it past the pip-squeak to sneak into Wade's trailer to get a quote.

He heard another noise, like someone trying to open his door. He swung out of his bunk and pulled on a pair of jeans. He might be bruised and battered, but he could still throw a punch, and he was in enough of a bad mood to do just that.

He jerked open the door, fist clenched. The last

person he expected to see standing in the American Royal parking lot was Anne Chatsworth.

His first thought was, Thank God she hadn't found him with Wendy. The blonde had made herself scarce after the accident. She'd wanted to sleep with a champion, not a has-been. His second thought was, What the hell did he care what Anne Chatsworth thought of him?

But he did care, damn it.

"What are you doing here?" he demanded.

"I love you."

Wade had been prepared to argue against anything but that. In fact, he didn't know how to react to her point-blank admission. At one time he'd longed to hear her say just that. Even now, even after what she'd done, his heart gave a little lurch at hearing the words.

"I was watching the rodeo on TV. I saw what happened. Oh, Wade, is Traveler all right?"

Traveler? *Traveler?* She'd come here because of his damn horse? That was the sweetest thing she could have asked.

"Traveler broke his leg."

Anne sobbed. "I know. You didn't—I mean, you don't have to—"

"He's still with us, if that's what you mean. Vet hauled him to his office. He's iced up and drugged up and feeling no pain at the moment."

She shivered, and he realized she wasn't wearing a jacket. He was shirtless himself, and the wind was downright icy.

"Is there anything I can do?" she asked. "I could help pay the vet bills. Whatever he needs. Or I could sit with him, rub his forehead the way he likes so he wouldn't be alone and scared.''

Wade had wanted to do the same thing, but the vet hadn't allowed it. ''Come inside before you freeze to death.'' He stood aside to allow her into his cramped living quarters. He got a whiff of her scent as she passed, and he almost lost it. He grabbed a flannel shirt from a peg and thrust his arms into the sleeves so he wouldn't feel so vulnerable.

He unfolded a pull-down chair for her, then sat on the edge of his bunk. All he could think about were the wild good times they'd had on that bunk during the Mesquite Rodeo last spring. The fact that it was barely big enough for one body, let alone two, hadn't bothered them in the least.

Anne folded her hands primly in her lap. He leaned his elbows on his knees. He stared at her, drinking in the sight of her.

After a long, awkward silence, she spoke. ''What are you going to do?''

Jeez, she was as bad as the reporter. ''I have no idea, okay? First I'm going to get my horse in good enough shape to travel. Then I guess I'll go home, regroup.''

''Home?''

Wade hadn't even realized he'd used that word. Strange, but he'd come to think of Cottonwood as home for the first time in thirteen years. ''To the ranch, I guess. Maybe I'll try ranching for a while. Jonathan will probably fight me the whole way.''

''You don't like ranching.''

''I can stand it for a couple of years. Without that

championship prize money, I'm a ways from being able to start my stud farm."

"Maybe I could help."

"No way!" he exploded. "We're talking more than a few thousand dollars here. Anyway, you can't just throw money at a problem to solve it. I won't let you buy me off just to soothe your guilty conscience."

"This is not about guilt!" she returned. "This is about wanting someone I love to see his dreams come true."

"Only one problem with that, Annie. My dreams include you—or at least, they used to. And your daddy's money can't fix that."

Her face softened. "No, it can't. And money can't fix the fact that I lied to you—or, at least, I wasn't completely honest. I have no excuse except I could not seem to push the words out of my mouth, no matter how noble my intentions."

He could have taken her in his arms then. He could have eased his pain and disappointment with Annie's warm body next to his. But to give in to such a temptation would only be setting himself up for more pain later. Her lack of honesty hurt.

"I did a lousy job of handling a painful situation," she said. "I'm not asking to be excused. I'm hoping I'll be forgiven."

Wade knew then he was at a crossroads. He had to forgive her, completely, right now, or they were doomed. They had to put this series of mistakes behind them once and for all—or end up dealing with bitterness down the road, just like with him and Jonathan.

Looking at her now, so penitent, her eyes brimming with tears, he realized he wasn't the only one feeling pain. Damn, hadn't he learned that lesson once in his life? Hadn't he realized every story had two sides, that the world didn't revolve around him and his perceived slights?

"Maybe I'm the one who needs forgiving."

"For what?"

"For running off in a huff like the hothead I am, instead of sticking around to talk things out."

She smiled tremulously. "We're talking now, and that's all that matters. Do you still...do you still want to be with me?"

Still he didn't trust himself to touch her, to hold her. "I want you, you know I do. But not for just a night or a week or even every other weekend."

"I don't want that, either. I want to be with you every night. I want to wake up next to you every morning."

Wade let a note of hope ring in his ears for a few seconds. What, exactly, was she saying? "You want me to come live in New York with you? Or Miami or Boston or wherever the hell you'll be working?"

She was shaking her head. "I'm not going to any of those places. My dad will have an apoplectic fit, but I've realized I'm not cut out for the life of a big-city attorney. I don't want to put my personal life on hold while I make money and climb the corporate ladder. I want to live now. Because who knows how long we have on this earth? When you and Traveler fell, when you didn't get up—my God, all I could think about was, what if I blew it? What if you were gone for good?"

She was talking very quickly now, and all Wade could do was stare and try to absorb the implications. Only in his wildest fantasies had he envisioned Anne Chatsworth saying this sort of stuff to him.

"I could set up an office in Cottonwood," she continued. "Maybe the town doesn't have enough legal business to keep me busy full-time, but that's okay. I'll learn to cook. Maybe I'll become a gardener. And maybe, if you'll let me, I'll help you run that stud farm. And if you decide to settle down somewhere else, well, I could go there, too. I think it's better to have family close by, even if you don't always get along, but I'll respect—"

"Anne, stop!"

"If you kick me out, I'll have to sleep in my car. There's not a hotel room left in town."

He had no intention of kicking her out. She'd all but melted his heart with her speech. Perhaps at one time she hadn't trusted him, but she must trust him a lot to throw her heart into his lap that way. To just march in here and tell him she loved him, after the way they'd left things in Cottonwood—that showed all kinds of courage.

He opened his arms. "Come here. Please."

When she hesitated, he stood, hauled her to her feet and put his arms around her. There wasn't anyplace for her to escape in his trailer, anyway.

"I'm sorry," he said. "I'm sorry I got so angry. I got no right to get mad just because you didn't handle your life exactly like I thought you should have. You must have been really scared and sad and upset. I can't blame you for being mixed-up and not knowing who to tell, who to trust."

She buried her face against his neck. He could feel the damp of her tears. "I should have told you. I was going to. But I knew, after seeing you with Sam and Kristin, after hearing how you wanted your own kids, I knew you'd take it hard. And I guess I just didn't want to see that. I didn't want to hurt you that way, even though not telling you ended up hurting you worse."

"It's okay now. It's all over," he soothed.

She squeezed him hard and he gasped in pain—the physical kind. "What?" she asked. Then, "Oh, my gosh, you're hurt, you're injured. Are you all right? You hit your head, you were unconscious, you were squashed by a horse—"

"It's about time you showed a little concern," he said when he could breathe without breaking into a sweat. "You were so worried about the damn horse, I was beginning to think *he* was the one you really wanted."

Anne refused to laugh. She climbed off his lap and examined his face for injuries, then parted his open shirt. She gasped when she saw the huge bruise forming there on his chest. "You should have gone to the hospital."

"I'm all right. Although if a few more injuries will get me the pity vote, I sprained my ankle, broke a rib and I have a concussion."

"Oh, Wade." She pointed sternly at his bunk. "You get back in bed this instant."

"Only if you come with me."

"I'm afraid I'll hurt you."

"Trust me, it'll hurt a lot worse if you stay away."

And he wasn't kidding. He either needed Anne or a cold shower.

She smiled. "Well, if you insist." She pulled her sweater off over her head, revealing only a thin, sleeveless undershirt. No wonder she'd been cold. He could see her nipples puckering beneath the see-through fabric.

Wade shucked his jeans, easing them carefully over his swollen ankle. It was black-and-blue, like his chest.

"Wade! You need to put ice on that and wrap it in a bandage."

He grabbed her by the waist of her jeans and pulled her closer. "Later, Nurse Annie. Right now, you're the only first aid I need." He unbuttoned her jeans and slid them over her hips, pleased to see that her bikini panties were as transparent as the undershirt.

He pulled her closer still and laid his cheek against her belly. To think there'd been a child growing there at one time—his child. But that was looking back, and now he only wanted to look toward his future—their future. She ruffled his hair, stopping to gently probe the goose egg on the back of his head.

"Are you sure you're up for this?" she asked, concern lacing her voice.

"Darlin', believe me, I'm *up*. Or do you need convincing?"

"You can convince me anytime."

He leaned into the bunk and pulled her with him, guiding her descent so she didn't fall on his sore ribs. She laughed as she kicked off her jeans and tennis shoes. "I'm still afraid I'll hurt you."

How could he tell her nothing would hurt as much

as this week without her? He didn't want to try. He just kissed her, long and hard, wrapping his arms around her securely.

She answered his kiss in kind, meeting his tongue with hers like a wanton siren, then covering his face with kisses like an eager puppy. She couldn't seem to make up her mind which she was.

"Are you really here to stay?" he asked, not quite believing.

A shadow crossed her face. "As long as you'll have me. Wade, there's something else I have to tell you."

Wade didn't want to talk anymore. He didn't want to think anymore. He just wanted to lose himself in the feel of Anne's body close to his, the delicate smell of her skin, the softness of her womanhood.

He kissed her again, more insistently. "Mmm, can't it wait?" Now he was the one delaying, but as long as she was staying with him, he didn't care about anything else.

She caressed his face, her expression far too serious for his peace of mind. "It can wait a few minutes. Make love to me, Wade."

That was one request he was pleased to comply with.

They loved each other slowly, savoring every moment. Wade appreciated Anne in a whole new way—knowing she loved him, knowing they were committed. He felt no more doubts, no more uncertainty. Whatever she had to tell him, even if it was bad news, they would weather it together.

With her lying on him, he stroked her thighs, gradually moving his hands until she understood his intent. She opened to him, letting him probe her sweet, warm center until she was gasping for breath. But he showed her no mercy, clasping her hard against him with one arm. Her ecstatic wiggling only excited him further.

When he'd teased her about as far as was practical, he lifted her hips and eased her over him. Her smile told him she was more than ready for him. She needed no coaxing to move in a rhythm that brought him far too quickly to a crescendo, but he didn't care. They'd do it all again later, even more slowly. He intended to discover every mystery Anne's body had to offer. And when they were both exhausted and sated, he would probe other mysteries—those of her heart.

He wanted to know everything about her, absolutely everything, so she could never surprise him again. Except he knew Anne would always hold mysteries, would always surprise him.

She groaned and sighed and maybe even shed a few tears as she climaxed, then relaxed against him, every muscle soft. His ribs hurt like hell, but he didn't care. As long as she was close to him he didn't care about anything.

A few minutes later she moved from atop him to beside him. The tiny bunk forced them to stay close, for which he was grateful. Who needed a king-size bed when Anne was here?

"I know it's late," she said. "I know you want to go to sleep. But we really do have to talk."

"I'm not sleepy. We can talk till dawn if you want."

"It's about the baby—our baby. We don't know

for sure, but Jeff thinks I miscarried because the baby had a genetic heart defect."

An unpleasant sensation crawled up Wade's spine. "There was something wrong with it?"

"Yes. I had a blood test. I've got a bad gene. It runs in my family—my mother had several miscarriages before I was born."

"Are you saying you can't have children?"

"I'm saying *we* can't have children...or, rather, there's a good chance we can't." She tried to sit up, but he wouldn't let her put distance between them.

"Stay right here, you're not going anywhere."

"If you have the same gene, Wade, it means we shouldn't have children. There's a very good chance that even if I carried a child full term, it might have a serious heart problem."

"Oh, Annie." He turned his head and kissed her cheek, tasting the salt of her tears. The very idea of losing another child horrified him. He couldn't even imagine how she felt, having gone through the loss of a child firsthand. "Oh, Annie, my poor darling girl. You've been carrying around this secret all this time. No wonder you didn't want to tell me."

"I won't blame you if you want to forget it—forget about us. I know how important having children is to you—"

He put his hand over her mouth. "Just stop right there. Sure, I love kids. But there are lots of ways to get kids without conceiving them the old-fashioned way. We could adopt. Or...or you could go to a sperm bank. I'm not that attached to my DNA."

He released her mouth, and she took a deep breath. "You mean it?"

"Of course I mean it. And in case I haven't made it clear lately, I do want to marry you."

"And I want to marry you—more than anything."

He kissed her again, sealing their bargain. Then, stifling a groan, he sat up. "Don't move." He got out of bed and rummaged around in a storage drawer under the bunk until he found what he was looking for. Then he opened the velvet case and presented his mother's necklace to Anne a second time.

This time, however, he wasn't even nervous. He was sure of her love, her commitment. He switched on a lamp so he could see to fasten the clasp.

"I'm sorry I was such an idiot at the restaurant, the first time you tried to give this to me."

"I understand about that now. It's okay. It's a story we'll tell our grandkids."

He put the necklace on her. It glimmered in the lamplight, the green fire exactly matching her eyes. "I think you should wear the necklace and nothing else all the time. Well, whenever we're alone, anyway. It looks like it was meant for you."

"Thank you, Wade. I hope your mother would approve of your choice."

"I know she would. She overcame a lot to marry my dad. She believed in love conquering all, even if they didn't exactly get their happily-ever-after."

"Me, too, Wade. Me, too."

They snuggled a few minutes in silence until Anne asked a sudden question. "If you don't ride Saturday night, that means you can't win the championship."

Wade sighed. "That's right. Hell, I didn't even need to win. Second or third place would give me the points I need."

"Then why not ride another horse?"

"What horse? Good calf-roping horses don't exactly grow on trees."

"What about Cimmy?"

Wade snorted. "She's not very well trained. Anyway, she's in Texas."

"Call Jonathan. Have him ship her up here."

"Anne, are you nuts?"

"What could it hurt? Cimmaron's got the instincts, you said so yourself. Maybe you'll bomb, but at least you could take a chance."

The idea was just crazy enough to try. "Jonathan won't cooperate."

"Try him. Call him first thing in the morning. Tell him you're getting married."

"I could tell him I'm coming home to work on the ranch. That ought to sway him."

"No, don't tell him that. If you win the championship, you won't need to work on the ranch. And if you don't win...well, Wade, I've got a ton of money. A trust fund."

"I can't let you—"

"A loan, then. We'll be partners, and that means partners in everything."

Wade just laughed and shook his head. His future wife was crazy, and what was worse, so was he.

He used Anne's cell phone to call Jonathan at dawn, knowing that was the only time he was likely to catch him at home. Workdays started early on the ranch.

"Hey, big bro. It's the prodigal son, Wade."

A long silence greeted him. Then, "Wade. This is a surprise. Are you okay?"

Jonathan had heard about the rodeo disaster, and Wade quickly filled him in on the details.

"Sorry to hear it," Jonathan said, sounding genuinely regretful. "I know that horse means a lot to you. Does this mean you lose the championship?"

Wade was surprised Jonathan even knew about that. "Yeah, probably. Unless you help me out."

"Me?"

"I know you don't owe me anything, but I wish you'd do me a big favor. I need you to load Cimmaron in a trailer and have somebody drive her up here. I want to compete with her Saturday night."

Jonathan didn't even question the harebrained decision. "I'll do it this morning. She'll be in Kansas City by this evening."

Wade was genuinely surprised. "Thank you, Jon."

"It's the least I can do." Jonathan cleared his throat. "Guess I was a little hard on you."

"A little?"

Anne, who was listening in, jabbed Wade in the ribs—the ones that weren't broken, thankfully.

"I was crazy when I thought I might lose Kristin," Jonathan continued. "I know it wasn't your fault. I know that now. I suspect I knew it then, but I was lashing out at anyone so I wouldn't have to blame myself."

"For what?" Wade asked, bewildered.

"For...I don't know. For not staying home with Kristin myself when she was sick. For leaving the kids with baby-sitters all the time. Hell, for losing their mother. Anyway, I hope you'll forgive me someday. Meanwhile, I'll send you the horse. And when you're ready, I hope you'll come home to Cottonwood—to visit or to stay, whatever. Sam and Kristin miss you. Hell, I miss you.''

Well, what do you know. Wade had never in a million years thought he'd hear those words from Jonathan.

''I miss y'all, too,'' Wade said, his throat thick. ''Oh, Jon, one more thing. Me and Anne are getting married.''

A long silence. Then, ''Well, lots of surprises for so early in the morning.''

ANNE'S HEARTBEAT wouldn't slow down at all the next day, her anticipation was so high. Maybe she was crazy to encourage Wade, still recuperating from his own injuries, to compete in the finals with Cimmaron. But if he didn't at least take a crack at it, he would always wonder if he could have won.

The rumor mill was buzzing with the news that Wade Hardison hadn't withdrawn from the finals tomorrow night and that he would compete on a brand-new, untested horse.

By the time the Hardison Ranch rig pulled into the parking lot of the American Royal, Wade was ready. He'd taped his ankle and ribs, and he'd arranged for some practice time late tonight in the ring, after everyone else was done for the day.

Anne was surprised when the driver's door opened and Jonathan himself climbed down.

''This was one show I couldn't miss,'' he said. The two brothers hugged awkwardly. Then Jonathan embraced Anne. ''Welcome to the family, and best wishes—you'll need them, marrying into our crazy clan.'' But the ribbing held not a hint of malice.

They all stayed up until the wee hours while Wade worked with Cimmy. Her performance was disastrous. She shot out of the gate like a bullet, but she never stopped in the right place, and more times than not she didn't stand still after Wade dismounted.

But about one run out of five she was flawless. She had potential. If Wade could just get lucky at the finals, he might accumulate enough points to win that prize money.

They all went to bed exhausted—but Wade and Anne weren't too tired to make love again. ''For luck,'' Wade said, but she didn't need any excuses.

Anticipation was high as the calf-roping finals got underway on Saturday night. Wade finagled some great seats for Anne and Jonathan, right in front. Anne was sure the suspense would finish her off. What if that silly horse made a fool of Wade? Or worse, what if Wade got hurt again? Why had Anne ever made such a crazy suggestion?

Wade was one of the last to compete. The calf was released, and it ran like the wind, a crazed look in its eyes. Cimmy and Wade bolted across the line, a single unit of muscle and determination. The lasso flew and Wade drew Cimmy up smartly, jerking the calf almost off its feet.

Wade dismounted without a hitch—giving the spirited horse a warning look, or so Anne imagined. Cimmy stood her ground, keeping the rope taut, as Wade wrapped the pigging strings around three of the calf's legs. He threw his hands up in the air to signal he was done, then climbed back on Cimmy.

Anne glanced at the clock. His time was good. Damn good.

The calf struggled mightily, and the crowd held its collective breath to see if the tie would hold for the required six seconds.

It did. A huge cry went up. Cimmy flipped out over the noise and reared up, then started bucking. But it didn't matter now. Wade got the young horse under control, then waved to the crowd. He guided the highly strung horse out of the ring, and Anne could tell by the look on his face that he knew he'd just become the national calf-roping champion.

Anne and Jonathan immediately went to find Wade. They could hardly get to him, there was such a crowd around him. Anne saw a well-endowed blonde throw her arms around him and give him a big smacking kiss. Wade seemed to enjoy the attention, but he set the woman away from him the moment he saw Anne.

He grinned sheepishly.

"Who in the heck was that?" she asked as she threw her own arms around him.

"Wendy. Jealous?"

"Yes."

"Don't be. It's not me she wants. It's that gold championship buckle that turns her on."

"I'm *so* comforted." Still, Anne found herself glad Wade was giving up competition. She didn't want blond floozies throwing themselves at him, even if he always and forever said no. She wanted him home, with her. And with their children, however they acquired them.

"I'd sleep with you even if you weren't national champion," Anne whispered in his ear.

"I will definitely take you up on that." He flashed

a smile just for her, and she slid a possessive arm around his waist. She had dibs on this cowboy, for tonight and forever. Annie would never run away again.

Epilogue

"Cut in closer!" Wade shouted. "Lean to the right. Get your hand off that saddle horn."

Wade smiled as his student, an eight-year-old girl named Mandy, wobbled her way around the barrel-racing course. When she'd arrived at the Cottonwood Rodeo Camp a week ago, she'd been terrified of horses. Now she was riding by herself, laughing with exhilaration as she urged Danny, Sam's gentle old horse, into a canter toward the finish line. Sam had recently graduated to a more spirited mount and had generously loaned Danny to Wade's camp.

Wade clicked off the stopwatch. "Forty-two seconds," he shouted. "That's twelve seconds better than last time." Mandy wouldn't win any blue ribbons with that time, but it didn't matter. She beamed like a lighthouse as she dismounted by herself and handed the reins to Len, one of the camp's teenage counselors.

Another little girl mounted the ever-patient Danny.

"Break for lunch in five minutes," Wade told Len before going to check on some of the older boys, who were learning how to rope a calf. The animal they were practicing on was an old hand, having dodged lassos in two previous camp sessions. It looked bored. Wade made a mental note to return it to Jonathan's herd and get a fresh calf that would run faster.

Wade heard a car engine coming up the long driveway. He felt a familiar tug of anticipation when he recognized the silver SUV headed his way. Anne had traded in the Mustang a few months ago for something more practical.

"Okay, that's it for now," he called to the ropers. "Looks like lunch is here."

The camp had hired Sally Enderlin as a cook, but on her days off it was Catch As Catch Can. Wade always appreciated it when Anne could swing by a barbecue place or pizza parlor and pick up food for the kids on her way home from work. After passing the bar exam, she'd set up a little storefront office in town next to Hollywood Lingerie. She'd generated enough work to keep her busy, especially when she started getting referrals from neighboring towns. But two weeks ago she'd started cutting back her hours to half days.

Anne pulled up next to the fence and climbed out, taking her time. Wade rushed over and gave her an assist. Two weeks from her due date, she looked as if she'd swallowed a beach ball. She always had trouble standing up, though she claimed to feel fantastic otherwise.

"Hello, gorgeous," he said with a smile, giving her a quick kiss. "You smell almost as good as that barbecue in the back seat. Ribs?"

"Of course. I've brought home enough for an army."

"I'll call some of the kids to carry it over to the pavilion."

A year into his venture, things were going better than he'd ever hoped. Pete had deeded the wooded land with the creek and swimming hole to him for one dollar. Wade had carved some riding trails through it. Then Sally had sold him her farm. She was tired of running it, she said. She'd moved to an easy-care facility in town, but as much time as she spent at the Hardison Ranch with Pete, Wade suspected she'd soon be giving up the apartment.

Wade and Anne had fixed up the house and filled the barn and pastures with horses—high-end breeding stock, with Traveler and Cimmy as the big stars, along with a few ponies and some gentle, older horses.

They put up some simple cabins in the woods for the campers, and a pavilion for meals. They'd turned the old foreman's cottage into a food-preparation area. Then they started running newspaper ads in Dallas and Houston for the rodeo camp and crossed their fingers.

The response had been incredible. Every session was full, with a waiting list. Wade was already thinking about expanding the facilities to allow for more campers, though he didn't want it so big that he couldn't get to know each kid. The children quickly became like family, and it was hard as hell at the end of each session to let them go home.

Pretty soon, though, he and Anne would have their own little calf roper. Wade had done the blood tests. As it turned out, he didn't have the heart-defect gene. They would never know why they'd lost their first child, but Anne's second pregnancy had proceeded without a hitch—not even morning sickness.

Two of the counselors carried the food to the pavilion. Wade brought a cooler full of drinks from the cottage, then they all sat together at the long picnic table, one very big, noisy family—at least for a few more days.

"This isn't exactly the life you expected, is it?" Wade said quietly to Anne as she helped little Andy Anderson clean up a spilled soda. "You thought by now you'd be working in some high-rise, dressed in a suit and heels every day, pulling in a six-figure income."

"That doesn't even sound appealing anymore. I don't know why I ever thought I wanted it. I guess cause my dad convinced me it was the best life a person could have. And the funny thing is, he couldn't wait to retire from it."

"He's pretty happy you changed your mind, though."

"Well, he's pretty excited his first grandchild will live five minutes away. He's still pushing me, though. Wants me to run for judge in a couple of years."

"So the two of you can run the whole town, I guess." Milton had won his bid for town council, and he loved to shake things up among the other, more complacent council members. "Judge Annie. Not a bad idea."

"Maybe in a few years, when all our kids are in school. Right now I want to just enjoy the baby and the campers and the horses. I finally feel like I belong somewhere."

"Me, too." That was an understatement. He

couldn't understand why it had taken him so long to figure out this was what he wanted—a home, a place to belong. Sure, he'd wanted to make his mark in the world, follow a dream. But a national championship and a stud farm would mean nothing without people to share it with—his brothers and father and grandfather, Anne and her family, the city kids, all of whom he wanted to adopt.

And the new baby, who they knew by now was a girl.

Wade wanted to teach her everything he knew, instill in her a love for the land and the animals and Texas and family, all the while knowing the kid would have her own dreams to follow.

"You have a very strange look on your face," Anne said.

Wade laughed. "I was thinking about the future."

"Why, when the here-and-now is so darn perfect?"

He kissed her soundly, ignoring the hoots and catcalls from the campers. "You said it, Annie."

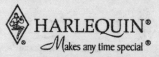

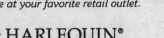

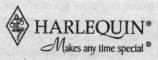

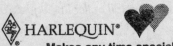

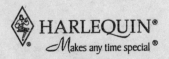